CHASING THE BRIDE

HEART & SOUL #2

ERICA RIDLEY

Heist Club:

The Rake Mistake

The Modiste Mishap

Rogues to Riches:

Lord of Chance

Lord of Pleasure

Lord of Night

Lord of Temptation

Lord of Secrets

Lord of Vice

Lord of the Masquerade

The *12 Dukes of Christmas*:

Once Upon a Duke

Kiss of a Duke

Wish Upon a Duke

Never Say Duke

Dukes, Actually

The Duke's Bride

The Duke's Embrace

The Duke's Desire

Dawn With a Duke

One Night With a Duke

Ten Days With a Duke

Forever Your Duke

Making Merry

Gothic Love Stories:

Too Wicked to Kiss

Too Sinful to Deny

Too Tempting to Resist

Too Wanton to Wed

Too Brazen to Bite

Magic & Mayhem:

Kissed by Magic

Must Love Magic

Smitten by Magic

Regency Fairy Tales

Bianca & the Huntsman

Her Princess at Midnight

Missing an Erica Ridley book?

Grab the latest edition of the free, downloadable and printable complete book list by series here:

https://ridley.vip/booklist

CHASING THE BRIDE

LORDS IN LOVE #6

ACKNOWLEDGMENTS

As always, I could not have written this book without the invaluable support of many others. Huge thanks go out to Darcy Burke, Elyssa Patrick and Erica Monroe. You are the best!

I also want to thank my wonderful VIP readers, our Historical Romance Book Club on Facebook, and my fabulous early reader team. Your enthusiasm makes the romance happen.

Thank you so much!

CHAPTER 1

London, 1818

*L*ady Tabitha Kerr stood just outside the door to her father's sickroom, trying to catch her breath. Although he had never been particularly demonstrative, her father was a good man. She knew this. It was why she had spent a lifetime trying her hardest to please him. And yet what the marquess was forcing his only child to do would confine Tabitha to a life of misery.

She rolled back her shoulders. She could no longer postpone the inevitable. She was a lady now. It was time to act like one.

Tabitha tapped her knuckles against the door. It opened instantly.

Mr. Hudson Frampton had beaten all other servants to the soft knock. Or else he'd been standing within reach of the handle, which was unlikely. Her betrothed's guard dog never left his employer's side, except to follow a direct order.

Mr. Frampton always seemed to be everywhere at once, and capable of absolutely anything.

At the moment, he was gazing at her gravely. His solemn expression did nothing to lessen his distracting handsomeness. He was no gentleman, and it showed. His brown hair was a little too long, his cravat creased carelessly, his strong jaw already shadowed with stubble at three o'clock in the afternoon. The omnipresent air of danger emanated from his conspicuous muscles.

He looked like a highwayman, not a viscount's man of business. Though perhaps the two roles were not so dissimilar. A highwayman robbed passing carriages. Lord Oldfield's infamous man of business had his fingers in every investment opportunity in London, often reaping greater rewards for the viscount than enjoyed by the poor souls who owned or executed the various operations.

"He's waiting for you," Mr. Frampton said softly, his dark brown eyes unreadable.

"Don't you mean *they're* waiting for me?" Lady Tabitha murmured, her correction tinged with bitterness. Viscount Oldfield might be Mr. Frampton's employer, but both men were in the sickroom of Tabitha's *father*.

Mr. Frampton's dark eyes glittered. "You are, of course, correct. My apologies."

"It's all right," she mumbled under her breath.

It was not all right. Life as she knew it would soon be over. The father she adored, dead. And the sly viscount of equally advanced age standing at the marquess's bedside... would soon own Tabitha outright, thanks to the legal glories of holy matrimony.

Mr. Frampton stepped aside to let her in.

Tabitha pasted on a smile and went straight to her father, passing both the odious Viscount Oldfield and the kindly physician Dr. Collins in her hurry to kiss her father's pale forehead and assure herself he would not be leaving her this day, at least.

"Daughter," the marquess rasped. "A welcome sight for sore eyes."

Her own eyes stung. That was one of the kindest things he had ever said to her. Perhaps confronting his mortality had likewise caused him to cherish the sole familial connection he had left.

"Always my pleasure, Father." She lifted his frail hand in hers and sent a questioning look toward the physician.

"Stable," Dr. Collins pronounced, loud enough for the marquess to hear. Then he dropped his white-whiskered mouth to Tabitha's ear. "But not for long. A month or two, at best. And at worst…"

She pulled her ear away before she could hear the rest of the good doctor's diagnosis. Tabitha patted her father's hand instead.

A wasting disease was one of the worst ways to die. It stretched on too long. Day after day of knowing death was coming, wiggling its hook in a little more with each passing breath.

It had been two months already. When her father was first diagnosed, they had thought the marquess might hold on for six more months, mayhap another year. But he grew weaker by the day and had been bed-bound for over a month, unable to rise without assistance. This past week, her father had ceased being able to feed himself. The effort of lifting a cup or a fork was too much. Every limb trembled, and every part of him ached.

Tabitha hated seeing him like this. He'd once been so vibrant. Afternoons spent fencing with his friends, or riding his favorite stallion in the park. As much as she appreciated having the opportunity to say goodbye, watching her father die a little more each day was torture.

For his sake, she wished a swift end to his suffering. But for *her* sake... Father's inevitable demise was the worst thing that could happen.

"You haven't... greeted your... betrothed," rasped the marquess.

Tabitha gritted her teeth behind a brittle smile and turned the pleasantest face she could muster toward Viscount Oldfield—who, it must be noted, had not greeted her either.

According to legend, such lack of manners was one of the many reasons their families had warred for generations. Both sides believed the other beneath them. Neither side was willing to bend.

Until Father. Bless him and curse him.

Tabitha did not curtsey to her betrothed. "Lord Oldfield. Please forgive my tardiness in greeting you."

The viscount ran his eyes over her as though he were imagining her naked. "Bah. I've no need for a wife who *talks*," he murmured, too low for her father to overhear.

Yes. This man thirty-plus years her senior desired her for reasons unrelated to conversation.

Such was her impending marital bliss.

She turned and dropped to her knees beside her father's sickbed. "Papa, surely you can see—"

"This union will heal a centuries-old rift," he reminded her, sensing the direction of her plea and putting a stop to it before she could embarrass them both in front of the viscount. "You should be proud to be a vessel of peace."

A vessel. That was exactly what she was going to be. A hard, empty vessel for Lord Oldfield to fill at his whim and to use as he saw fit.

Such unceasing attentions might break her.

"He's a *lord*," the marquess said hoarsely. "You should be grateful I've given you to such a fine friend. You might recall that Oldfield saved my life. I can never fully repay him for that. From the moment he and I first guarded the trenches together—"

Another war story. Heaven save her, Lady Tabitha had heard them all, dozens or hundreds of times each.

Father and Viscount Oldfield had met as British soldiers stationed together in the French revolutionary war, in the early 1790s. They'd both been raised to despise the other's family, but nonetheless had become unlikely friends, united against a common foe. And when it had mattered most, Oldfield had been there for the marquess.

"He's like a brother to me," Father continued.

Tabitha wanted to scream, *You wouldn't betroth your daughter to your brother, much less whilst still in the womb*, but she held silent. It didn't matter what she said. Father was the marquess, and his word was law.

"Besides," her father said gently. "You've always

hated to see people upset or at odds. Your marriage will wipe clean a century of bigotry and prejudice. You should be proud to play such an important role, daughter. You love to restore peace. And a titled match makes you the envy of your peers. You have better fortune than most."

Yes, yes, all of that was true, but...

Still on her knees at her father's side, Tabitha cast a despairing glance up at Viscount Oldfield. He leered at her, displaying the multicolored teeth jockeying in his mouth. He'd lost several in the war. All of which had been replaced by teeth scavenged from the French corpses littering the battlefield.

She would get to think of *that* every time the viscount kissed her.

Tabitha shuddered. She couldn't help it.

"It's your turn to serve the greater good, daughter." Father tilted his head toward the viscount. "Can you procure a special license?"

"No!" Tabitha scrambled to her feet. "I cannot marry yet. I'm not ready. This is… It isn't a good time. In fact, I won't have a free moment for a fortnight. I'm…" What could she conceivably be doing that would be more important than marrying a viscount? "I-I've already promised to attend the May Day festival in Marrywell. It lasts a week, and I must leave by morning to arrive for the opening ceremony."

Father held her gaze, then cast his exhausted eyes up toward Dr. Collins. "If we read the banns first, what are the chances I will live long enough to attend the wedding ceremony?"

Tabitha sagged with relief—and guilt. She did

not wish to disappoint her father or to cause him pain. A good daughter knew her duty and fulfilled it without question. Was she being selfish by not rushing into an unwanted marriage with a lecherous roué over twice her age?

"Shall you last another three weeks, milord? I should think so," said the physician. "You're not quite at death's door yet."

"But I have arrived outside its residence," the marquess said dryly, only to be wracked by a rattling cough.

Viscount Oldfield jerked his gaze toward his attack dog. "Hudson, see that the first banns are read tomorrow."

Mr. Frampton nodded. "It will be done."

Lady Tabitha let out her breath. The banns would be read three consecutive Sundays. Fifteen days total, from the first reading to the last. It was not much of a reprieve, but it was at least something.

"Oldfield," rasped the marquess. "Procure a special license as well. If I should worsen faster than expected…"

Tabitha swallowed. Her final fortnight of freedom would be curtailed in a second if there was cause to believe her father unable to hold on for the full reading of the banns.

"Consider it done," Mr. Frampton assured both men, without looking at Tabitha.

The marquess's pale blue eyes found his daughter. "Daughter…"

"I know, Father," she murmured. "I promise to make you proud."

Even if it destroyed any hope of her own happiness.

Seeing his only child wed to his old comrade-in-arms was the marquess's literal dying wish. The marriage *would* bring peace after generations of fighting. And the promise had already been made.

Only a monster would prioritize her own selfish preferences above the wishes of her dying father and the peace and happiness her sacrifice would bring future generations.

She sighed. A daughter's duty was to her father. Any other, less privileged young lady wouldn't even view this marriage *as* a sacrifice. Viscount Oldfield was wealthy and titled. An unattainable dream, for most. A coup Tabitha had lucked into from birth, no effort required. She was fortunate. The envy of debutantes everywhere, who would take her place at the altar in a heartbeat.

Tabitha wished she could let them.

"As it happens," said Viscount Oldfield, as he resumed his open leering, "I have plans to attend the May Day festival as well."

Oh no.

The viscount dipped his eyes toward Tabitha's bodice. "You can ride with me."

An eight-hour drive trapped in a private carriage with *him*? Untenable.

"Of course," the viscount continued, "I cannot leave until Wednesday—"

Tabitha seized on the opening. "I cannot wait that long. I've several appointments to keep, and must be off at first light. I'm very sorry the timing doesn't—"

Viscount Oldfield gestured at Mr. Frampton. "Go with her."

"What? There's no need to send your—" *Attack dog.* "—man of business," she protested. "Mr. Frampton belongs with you. Besides, I already have a maid. One who is well-versed in playing chaperone."

"Tabitha," gasped the marquess. "Do as your future husband commands. You will soon vow to love and obey him. It wouldn't hurt to start practicing that obedience now."

She ground her teeth behind a tight smile. "Very well. I'll take Mr. Frampton. We'll meet you at the festival, Lord Oldfield."

His eyes still hadn't left her bodice. "See that you do."

Tabitha nodded woodenly. Her fortnight of freedom had become anything but free. Instead, she was trapped.

Tomorrow's long journey was the beginning of the end.

CHAPTER 2

$\mathcal{E}$arly the next morning, Hudson was responding to the last of the investment requests on his desk when the bell on the wall tinkled, summoning him to his employer's bedchamber.

In most houses, such requests only rang in the downstairs servants' area, usually upon a wall of bells and cords near the kitchens. Someone was always stationed to watch and listen, and dispatch servants as necessary. Viscount Oldfield, however, never wished to be more than a tug of a bell pull away from his man of business.

As usual, Hudson ignored the call. He would go to his employer soon enough—Hudson always did —but not before he finished writing his response to the latest proposal to cross his desk. This opportunity would make him and the viscount both significantly richer, the latter of which would please his employer.

And as for pleasing Hudson…

Lord Oldfield had no notion that Hudson invested most of his earnings in the same stocks and investment opportunities that he procured for his employer. How would he? The viscount didn't attend to his correspondence at all. He trusted Hudson to manage everything from financial concerns to social invitations.

Hudson did so with aplomb. He was rewarded handsomely for his talent and effectiveness. And since he had no particular expenses of his own—meals and a private suite were provided for him in each of the viscount's residences—why *not* invest his wages and grow rich alongside his employer?

He rang for a footman to deliver the latest round of signed contracts, then strode upstairs to the viscount's private quarters. If Hudson was not mistaken, his employer had just arrived home from his usual carousing at his gentlemen's club, followed by a visit to a brothel or two.

As expected, Lord Oldfield was disheveled and clearly in his cups.

"Have you left for Marrywell yet?" the viscount slurred.

"I'm to collect your bride in a quarter hour," Hudson replied. "Are you certain you don't wish to accompany us?"

"Bah, I can tup her all I wish in a few weeks' time. But tonight..." Lord Oldfield swayed forward, his whiskey-laced breath fetid. "I found a pair of whores I like at Vauxhall. They're sisters, and—"

"Oh, dear." Hudson made a show of peeking at his pocket watch. "I would love to hear all about it, but I'll be late if I don't make haste. Was there something else you wanted?"

The viscount blinked at him in confusion. "Did I summon you?"

"Go to bed," Hudson suggested. "Sleep it off. Your whores will still be waiting for you when you awake."

"That's what my valet said," Lord Oldfield mumbled, then shut the door in Hudson's face.

Ah, the joys and dignity of working for the viscount.

Hudson checked his pocket watch again. If he left now, he'd be half an hour early. Something told him he ought not to delay, or the beautiful Lady Tabitha might "accidentally" set out without him.

The carriages were ready. One for Hudson and the young lady, and the other for their traveling trunks and footmen. He passed by his suite to pick up his hat, and then headed across Mayfair to Lord Brigsby's residence.

When he arrived, Lady Tabitha was just emerging from the marquess's town home with her lady's maid.

As always, Hudson's throat went dry at the sight of Lady Tabitha.

Glossy black hair piled in artful ringlets. Startlingly blue eyes framed by inky lashes. Plump, rosy lips. Plump everything, just as Hudson liked it. Voluptuous curves a man could get lost in for days. Wrapped up in a sunny yellow day dress decorated with flirty white ribbons and little embroidered rosettes along the hem. He wanted to pull her into his arms and cover those gorgeous lips with his own.

He did no such thing, of course.

"Not leaving without me, are you?" Hudson asked lazily, as he dropped down from the viscount's carriage.

Lady Tabitha looked guilty, then irritated, then resigned, all in the space of a second.

"Of course not," she muttered, waving a gloved hand to signal her driver to take her father's coach-and-four back to the stables. "That would be unforgivably rude of me."

"Splendid." Hudson held open the door to the viscount's third-nicest carriage. Lord Oldfield had kept the best ones for himself. "After you, then."

She allowed him to hand her into the coach. "Mary Frances comes with me."

"Of course." Hudson handed up her lady's maid as well.

He took the rear-facing seat so that the women would have the better view and more comfortable ride, and tapped the driver's panel above his head to alert the coachman that they were ready for departure.

The horses clopped into motion.

Hudson touched the rim of his top hat. "May I?"

"Of course," Lady Tabitha murmured.

He removed his hat and placed it on the seat beside him.

The two women exchanged an inscrutable glance, culminating in a shrug by Lady Tabitha. Mary Frances reached for the ribbon under her mistress's chin, but Lady Tabitha brushed her maid's hand away. "I can untie my own bonnet, thank you."

Soon, both bonnets and both pelisses lay next to the top hat at Hudson's side.

Nonetheless, Lady Tabitha did not look more comfortable. She looked as though she'd happily murder Hudson and dive out the closest window, scampering to safety like a frightened bunny evading a wolf.

"So that we're clear," he said, "I've no wish for any acrimony between us."

Lady Tabitha looked startled. "Acrimony?"

"My mission is twofold," he explained. "To protect you on this journey and to deliver you safely to Lord Oldfield."

Her jaw visibly tightened. "Much obliged, I'm sure."

"Other than that," he continued gently, "you may say and do anything that you please. You shall enjoy the same confidentiality that I grant to my employer. And as much freedom as I am allowed to offer you."

Lady Tabitha's brow furrowed slightly. She tilted her head as if she had never before considered the notion that Hudson would be as loyal to her as he was to his employer. *Or* had ever realized that Hudson found their arranged match just as distasteful as he suspected Lady Tabitha herself felt.

"Your first loyalty is to my betrothed," she said slowly.

"As will yours soon be," he agreed. "However, that does not mean either one of us ceases to be a whole person with our own lives and wishes."

"Very true." She was now staring at him openly, as though seeing him for the first time.

It was not the first time they had stood in each other's sights. Possibly not even the three-hundredth time.

Hudson had come to work for the viscount eight years ago, at the age of twenty. Two years would need to pass before Lady Tabitha turned sixteen and had her official come-out. But because of Lord Oldfield's ties to the Marquess of Brigsby, the viscount—and by extension, his omnipresent man of business—were frequent fixtures at the Brigsby household. Hudson had glimpsed Lady Tabitha for the first time within a month of his employment to the viscount.

It was not love at first glance. She would barely look anyone in the eyes, so shy was she in those days. Coltish limbs, too-large features she would later grow into. A father with enough money to grant her every wish… but without a heart big enough to.

"You don't want to marry him," Hudson observed quietly.

Lady Tabitha's eyes flashed with anger. "I am a dutiful daughter."

"An excellent side-step, and perhaps the answer to my question." He leaned back against the squab and folded his arms over his chest.

She glared at him. "Aren't you at least going to tell me I'm overreacting, and that I shall no doubt be quite happy as Viscountess Oldfield?"

Hudson arched an idle brow. "Are you? Will you?"

"No and no," muttered Mary Frances.

Lady Tabitha dug an elbow into her maid's

ribs, then turned back to Hudson. "Shouldn't you at least pretend to try and convince me?"

"Why would I? You have eyes and ears and at least a modicum of sense. You're old enough to make your own decisions. And I'm not paid to lie to you."

She blinked. "It's rude to… confirm my impending misery."

"I am sorry you'll have to face it."

"So 'sorry' that you'll consign me to my fate anyway, by force if necessary, because that *is* what you're paid to do."

Hudson inclined his head. "I do have my orders. Don't you?"

CHAPTER 3

$\mathcal{A}$ tortured look crossed Lady Tabitha's face. She blinked rapidly and turned to the window, as if pretending Hudson hadn't spoken.

He could have done the same. He watched her from beneath his lashes instead. When she was this near, he never could tear his gaze away. Hell, not even if she were on the opposite side of a crowded ballroom.

No, it had not been love at first sight. All things took time. Hudson couldn't really say when the change had occurred. One day, his employer's betrothed was a gangly, timid adolescent, and the next she was... Lady Tabitha, extraordinary beauty. Fully grown woman.

Shyness had given way to stoicism. She had indeed always been a dutiful daughter. Lady Tabitha was also a rose of polite society. Pleasant, elegant, always proper. He'd heard any number of people say she would make any lucky lord the perfect wife.

Unfortunately for her, the only lord she had to choose from was Viscount Oldfield.

Hudson couldn't blame any man for wishing to marry her. Not even the viscount. Lady Tabitha was sweet and clever and kind and biddable.

If Hudson could change just one thing about her, it would be that last one. To the devil with duty and subservience! In her boots, Hudson would drown himself in a bucket of tea before he'd voluntarily deliver himself to Lord Oldfield's bed. God save her, the viscount's wedding gift to his bride was bound to be a raging case of syphilis.

"Will you continue to visit Marrywell in future years?" Hudson asked.

Lady Tabitha arched a thin black eyebrow. "Attend a matchmaking festival after I'm married?"

"Both of you have attended multiple times, despite already being betrothed to each other," he pointed out.

She tilted her head and made a small smile that did not reach her eyes. "I am not certain how much my intended registered my presence."

Ah. So she *was* somewhat aware of her future husband's… proclivities.

"I am confident you did not escape the viscount's notice," Hudson forced himself to reply.

Lord Oldfield would never waste an opportunity to ogle his betrothed… or to angle after any other pretty young miss who wandered into his sights. At least whilst the marquess wasn't around to witness his behavior.

Hudson was not interested in the other women. He could not look away from Lady Tabitha. Even when he closed his eyes, she haunted his dreams. Not that he could ever let her know. A highborn lady like her would never dally with a lowborn commoner like him. To pretend otherwise would be to open himself to heartbreak —and immediate dismissal from his post.

"I suppose the better question is whether you would *wish* to continue attending the festival," he clarified.

"Do my wishes signify?" Lady Tabitha sent him a dry look. "I am informed that once I marry, the events I do or do not attend will be up to my husband's discretion."

And to think, such were the lives of Hudson's "betters". As far as he was concerned, it was better to be a peasant unfettered by such strictures.

If Hudson ever took a wife, he hoped she'd give him hell whenever he deserved it—and that by sunset, they would find their way back into each other's arms.

"I hope that you find more control over your future than you feel you have at this moment," he said. "No one deserves unhappiness."

Lady Tabitha's gaze snapped to his. "And what, precisely, do I deserve?"

A life of joy. A husband who worships you. Nights filled with torrid pleasure. The freedom to make your own decisions, for better or for worse. A husband who supports you in all of it.

"You deserve whatever it is that you want," he answered simply.

For a moment, her eyes looked haunted. Then the expression cleared, and her face lit with a genuine smile that warmed him to the marrow.

"And if I want… an elephant?" she asked at last, her tone teasing.

He smiled back. An elephant had famously

crossed the frozen Thames a few years ago during the most recent Frost Fair. "Simple enough to achieve, I'd imagine. If you want an elephant, save your pin money and purchase one. Or a trio of the beasts, if you'd rather."

"I *have* saved quite a bit of pin money over the years. How much does a good elephant cost?"

"My apologies, madam. You appear to have mistaken me for an elephant broker. This poor man of business can only procure you a variety of wild hares and the occasional wayward mouse."

She touched the ringlets tumbling from her coiffure. "I already have plenty of wild hairs, thank you very much. I should, perhaps, take you up on that mouse. I can always release it in defense, should my future elephant grow out of hand."

"A wise plan," he agreed. "You can carry the mouse in your empty reticule, since your pin money will have been depleted to purchase the elephant."

"You vastly underestimate how spoilt the only child of a wealthy marquess actually is," she said dryly. "I could fit an elephant *inside* a reticule large enough to hold my pin money. If you'd like, I could buy both of us each an elephant."

"That's a marvelous idea. We could race them on Rotten Row in Hyde Park."

"Do elephants race?"

"They do when chased by wayward mice," he assured her. "I'll bring several along in *my* reticule."

"Men ought to carry reticules," she agreed. "They're ever so practical."

"And yet, pockets would be more practical."

"Do you think my skirts have no pockets?" She fluffed her voluminous gown. "Dear sir, I might actually *have* an elephant hidden between the folds of all this material."

Hudson wouldn't mind diving beneath those skirts in search of it. Or any other treasures she'd like to direct him to.

"Let me know if you need help looking for it," he murmured, then immediately regretted his flippant words. Bawdy flirtation was for barmaids at the local tavern, not the polished young lady promised to Hudson's employer.

Lady Tabitha simply laughed. "I'll keep my menageric to myself for now, if you don't mind."

For now. Hudson's chest caught. Surely she didn't mean that the way every rapid beat of his heart *wished* she meant it. The idea that she might look at him with even a fraction of the desire he shared for her... No, he didn't mind one whit.

He sent her a crooked grin. "You are a woman of many surprises."

"Surprises? You don't know the half of it. My first surprise came before I was even born."

Hudson grimaced at the archaic practice of betrothing children. "Your father should at least have let you grow old enough to make the decision for yourself."

"You don't know much about the aristocracy if you think women are encouraged to make their own decisions," she said wryly.

"I was *just* thinking how much better off I am than you are," he agreed.

She looked surprised. "Better off? You? But I needn't work!"

"There's absolutely nothing wrong with meaningful employment. And trust me, wages count as meaningful. Besides, I'd argue that you've been employed far longer than I have. Your elephant-sized pin money didn't come for free, did it? That's your blood money for your unwanted betrothal."

She shook her head. "If you're right, then I am not an idle young lady after all, but a servant vastly underpaid for my labor."

"Is it untrue? No quantity of gold or elephants could compel me to wed against my will."

Her eyebrows flew up. "Have I ever said my impending marriage was against my will?"

Hudson snorted. "When the betrothal predates your birth, it wasn't your choice, by definition. Besides, can you look me in the eyes and honestly state that if you had your wish of marrying any person in the entire world, the man you'd choose would be Viscount Oldfield?"

She lifted her chin. "Against one's will and not being first choice are two completely separate things, don't you think? For example, I rise when Mary Frances shakes me awake, despite much preferring to burrow under the covers and continue sleeping."

"Why does she wake you so early, then?"

"Because I ask her to. I want to rise early and I don't want to do so, all at the same time. What a person wants is not always so linear."

He had the feeling she was trying to distract him. "To be clear, are you saying you *do* wish to marry my employer?"

"I'm saying…" She trailed off and cast her gaze

out the window for a long moment before collecting herself. "I'm saying, there's more to it than what I might desire. You know as well as I do that this union will reunite two powerful families after generations of sparring. It is a *good* thing. And… it is my father's dying wish."

Yes. That last one, more than anything. Hudson suspected Lady Tabitha's father could have asked his only child to turn herself *into* an elephant, and Lady Tabitha would have moved heaven and earth in hopes of finding a way to achieve the transformation.

She was a good daughter. A good person. She'd make the viscount a wonderful wife.

And she'd make herself miserable while she was at it.

CHAPTER 4

Two days later, Tabitha tried and failed to hide a snicker behind her ungloved hand.

"Are you laughing at me?" Mr. Frampton narrowed his eyes at her, then choked down the bite he was eating and chased it with a gulp of ale. "That was *not* the pie that won the competition, was it?"

She tried to blink at him innocently, but burst into laughter instead. "Last place, I'm afraid."

"Good God." He shoved his mostly untouched plate onto the closest passing tray. "Are you certain it was fit for human consumption?"

"I promise nothing." She grinned at him. "Want to unburden your soul with any last-minute confessions?"

"I confess to being one greasy crumb away from throttling you," he growled, and lifted two clawed hands as though to strangle her.

Tabitha danced out of reach, giggling. She could not recall the last time she'd had this much *fun* at a social event. Oh, she had friends, each of whom she only saw for a minute at a time here and there, between dances or at the dressmaker's or while waiting for a musicale to begin. But the past two days with Mr. Frampton had far surpassed the amount of time she'd ever spent in the company of someone who was neither a family member, nor the paid servant of one.

Yes, yes, Mr. Frampton was her future husband's man of business, and therefore still under *someone*'s employ… but rather than tag along at a respectful distance as Tabitha's maid was wont to do, Mr. Frampton cleaved to her side with a wholly irreverent lack of proper distance, as though they were two friends enjoying the festival together.

Or as though they were… a suitor and the object of his affection.

Nonsense, of course. At least, the suitor bit. Mr. Frampton was being paid to shadow her every step, not doing so due to the tender sensibilities of his besotted heart.

But as for friends? Tabitha was surprised to discover that designation could easily be true, if their circumstances had been different. Mr. Frampton was easy to talk to and a riot to walk through town with. She was having fun. A sensation she had despaired of ever feeling again.

Mr. Frampton had been ordered to ensure her safety, not to maintain propriety, which meant in addition to all of the regularly scheduled Marrywell festival events, Tabitha had also visited a race track, two gambling rooms, and three delightfully common taverns.

They were now in the botanical gardens, along with at least half of the other merrymakers in town. The wooden dais where the May Queen and King were crowned and various competitions occurred was to her left. The entrance to the enormous hedgerow labyrinth was to her right. She and Mr. Frampton were in the middle, where rows of tables had been set up for the various chefs and home cooks to sell samples of their wares.

Apparently, he would not be purchasing more of the competition-losing lamb shank pie.

"You are dreadful," he informed her. "A polite young lady would never hoodwink an unassuming man of business."

"You assume quite a lot," she returned with a cheeky smile. "Such as whether I am a polite young lady."

"Gloves off, are they?" He gave a wolfish smile. "Shall I select a sweet for my sweet?"

"Absolutely not," she said in haste, though her cheeks heated with pleasure. "After that pie, I don't trust anything you might try to feed me."

"I should have been just as suspicious of *your* motives," he grumbled.

"Shall we find the follies?"

She wanted to link her arm through his, but refrained. The truth was, she did not need to hold onto Mr. Frampton's elbow to find the follies. She knew Marrywell as well as her own slipper. She simply felt comfortable with Mr. Frampton.

However, Tabitha had no doubt that were she to make the demand, Mr. Frampton would hang back with her lady's maid and allow her to fraternize with the other merrymakers without intervention or interruption.

The problem was, she *liked* his interventions and interruptions. These past two mornings, she had bounded out of bed more excited to see Mr. Frampton's handsome face and hear whatever nonsense he might choose to spout, than she was interested in the actual matchmaking activities.

And… that interest seemed mutual. Already, Mr. Frampton had gleaned more about her in two days than her betrothed had bothered to ascertain in all of Tabitha's twenty-two years.

If only Viscount Oldfield were Mr. Frampton, and Mr. Frampton the viscount! It would be no hardship at all to imagine herself spending the rest of her days with someone who listened and who made her laugh. She hadn't even realized how fundamental those two characteristics were until she experienced them for the first time with Mr. Frampton, and realized just what she would be losing when they were gone.

Yet, Tabitha had no room to complain by most people's standards. She was highborn and privileged, with powerful friends and an endless supply of pin money. And she needn't even exert herself in the marriage mart to find herself engaged to an equally wealthy lord.

It was the stuff of fairy tales. In theory.

"You're making a dark expression," Mr. Frampton told her. "You didn't try the poisoned pie, did you?"

She shook her head. "Just thinking about…" *my future husband.*

Perhaps it wouldn't be as bad as she feared.

Yes, she well knew of Lord Oldfield's "lecherous old roué" reputation, but perhaps that would change after he became a married man. Perhaps he would take true interest in his new bride, beyond the contours of her bodice. Perhaps he would prove himself to be just as witty and kind and clever as his man of business. Perhaps she and Viscount Oldfield might actually fall in love. Or at least enjoy a modicum of mutually pleasurable companionship.

And perhaps Tabitha would give birth to a litter of flying elephants right here on the well-trodden grass.

CHAPTER 5

*H*udson and Lady Tabitha strolled through the crowded botanical gardens. Not arm-in-arm. A servant touching a lady in such a manner would not be proper—or wanted. But they did walk side-by-side, her expensive skirts occasionally brushing against the black leather of his Hessians.

Although he knew he should not entertain such ludicrous notions, Hudson could not help but wish Lady Tabitha was in his company because she chose to be, not because she had been ordered to put up with a bodyguard.

To be fair, she did not treat him like a nuisance... or even like a lesser. Despite her aristocratic heritage and his working class status—which itself was a significant step up from his impoverished roots—Lady Tabitha had not only accepted Hudson's presence, but even went so far as to treat him... rather like a friend.

Oh, obviously she could not introduce him as such to her peers or waltz with him at balls as though he were worthy of vying for her hand. But

Lady Tabitha stayed by Hudson's side, rather than force him to trail her from the shadows. Their conversations were lighthearted and easy, despite the circumstances looming over her.

Had she been peevish, Hudson would have understood. Had she been haughty, that would have been her right. But instead she was gracious and friendly and kind.

Hudson hoped his employer realized just what a treasure the viscount's betrothed was.

"There's to be dancing here in the gardens later this evening," Lady Tabitha said. "I should like to attend."

"Of course. We'll go at the time of your choosing, and I'll stay within eyeshot, should you need anything."

She tilted her head. "You do know that you could dance, too, if you wished?"

He met her gaze. "I am not on holiday. I am under the employ of the Viscount Oldfield."

Her eyebrows lifted. "Twenty-four hours a day?"

He shrugged. "Same as any other."

She frowned. "Does he allow you no time at all for yourself?"

"What do I need time for?" he asked lightly.

"Dancing, for one." Her answer was flippant, but her expression was serious.

"I don't dance."

This was only partially true. The fact of the matter was, Hudson would eagerly dance every song the orchestra played—if he could do so with Lady Tabitha.

In theory, Marrywell was the one place on

earth where such an unlikely event might actually happen. The matchmaking festival was known for uniting lovers across backgrounds and class lines. If Hudson weren't accompanying his employer's betrothed, a fair portion of the crowd would have no objection to him standing up for a dance with any woman willing to concede twenty minutes of her time.

But Lady Tabitha *was* already promised elsewhere. And Hudson *was* employed by her intended to look after her well-being and nothing more.

"Well, if a country maiden catches your eye and you change your mind…" Her voice lowered and her eyes sparkled. "I promise not to tell your employer."

The only woman he had eyes for was Lady Tabitha. It had been that way for years, and Hudson feared it would forever be so, even after she became Lord Oldfield's wife. But he did not wish to think about her future matrimony. For now, the two of them were on their own—likely for the one and only time in their lives. Viscount Oldfield would intrude soon enough. Hudson didn't wish to waste a single moment of his limited time with Lady Tabitha.

"The dancing isn't until this evening," he said instead. "What would you like to do this afternoon?"

She bit her lip and glanced about the botanical gardens. As beautiful as the flowers were, the grounds were too vast to cover in a single day, and they had already walked amongst the colorful blooms for nearly two hours.

"Something else," she said. "Something different."

He raised his brows. "Like what? Shall we gamble away your fortune? Join a circus? Hold up a stagecoach?"

She pretended to consider his outlandish suggestions, then shook her head shyly. "Could we visit the animals in the livestock tents?"

Hudson would wrangle a lion for her with his bare hands, if she asked. Of course he would accompany her to a livestock tent. Not for the first time, he wondered just what her life was like under her father's thumb to make her think a request so simple might not be granted.

And whether she would fare any better once she was leg-shackled to the viscount.

"We shall visit the livestock without further delay," he assured her, taking the first path in that direction. "Are you more fond of cows, sheep, or pigs?"

"My only encounters with any of them are when they're served at the dinner table," she admitted. "I've never been on a farm."

"But you've visited the livestock at previous festivals, at least?"

"No," she said softly. "Father considers cattle too rustic for a lady."

He stared at her in disbelief. "You've never seen a *cow*?"

Her cheeks flushed prettily. "Barns are dirty and farmers are common. I was instructed to remain amongst my peers in the gardens or the assembly rooms at all times."

In other words, visiting the livestock tent was a

minor rebellion. Possibly the first she'd ever undertaken. Hudson could not imagine being so sheltered as to think pigs and sheep exotic animals, but he was absolutely determined to grant her any desire he was capable of.

"Follow me to adventure," he informed her gallantly.

She gave him a grateful smile. "Thank you."

His heart melted. How could anyone possibly deny such a simple request? Hudson supposed his disbelief was precisely why their class lines could never cross. He didn't see anything wrong with dirt and cattle. He *was* common. The fact that he could not imagine her world proved he didn't belong anywhere near it.

Just like she would never fit in his world.

He escorted her into the first tent with more than a little trepidation. The clouds of dirt dusting up from their boots and the heavy air thick with the pungent scent of animals in close quarters had never bothered him before. But would it send Lady Tabitha running now?

He glanced down at her.

Her eyes were wide and shining. If she was offended by the smells or appalled by the dirt, she gave no sign.

"Look," she whispered, pointing. "*Sheep*. Why, they're huge!"

Hudson could not hide his grin. If she found these ordinary sheep bigger than expected, he could not wait for her to realize just how large cows could be.

"Let's take a closer look," he suggested.

"Can we?"

"I don't see why not. That's what they're here for. All of the animals are on display."

"Show me." She grasped his arm without seeming to realize she was doing so.

Hudson felt the touch through every stitch of his clothing. He hoped she'd never let him go.

"This way. There are even contests to determine which of these beasts is the best of all its peers."

She sent a surprised look up at him, her eyes filling with laughter. "Like the May Day king and queen?"

"But without the thrones, or crowns of flowers," he conceded.

"It sounds lovely." She peered over the railing at the milling sheep. "They look so soft. Do they bite?"

Before Hudson could reply, the farmer in the pen strode up to greet them. "Did I hear you say you'd like to touch one of my beasts?"

"Oh!" Lady Tabitha stammered. "I... All I meant was..."

The farmer made a low, wheedling sound and a young sheep with a black face and thick white wool waddled over to the side of the railing. "Go on, then. This is Chicory."

"Chicory," she repeated softly, stretching hesitant fingers over the wooden railing just far enough to graze the sheep's wooly flank. Lady Tabitha turned wide, delighted eyes toward Hudson. "She's *soft*. Not scratchy at all!"

"The older the animal, the coarser the fleece," the farmer explained. "Chicory is eight months old."

"Eight months! Then she has plenty of wool-making years ahead of her."

"And milk and cheese," agreed the farmer. "Unless a butcher buys her."

Lady Tabitha snatched her hand back from the railing. "You can't *eat* her!"

Hudson laughed. "Didn't you tell me your previous experience with livestock was limited to the appearance of meat at your dinner table? You do realize that all such meals were once animals like this one."

She looked so horrified, he felt bad for teasing her.

"It's all right," he assured her, then turned to the farmer. "How much are you selling Chicory for?"

"Don't eat her," Lady Tabitha begged, her voice strangled.

The farmer named a price.

Hudson withdrew a coin from his pocket. "Rather than take her home with us, if I pay your fee, can you promise us Chicory will be allowed to live a long and full life?"

The farmer shrugged. "It's your money."

Hudson handed the coin over. "Take good care of her."

"Thank you for saving her," Lady Tabitha whispered, gazing up at him as though he'd single-handedly vanquished an invading army, rather than spared the life of a single sheep.

He smiled at her. "Any time."

She took his arm again as they crossed to the next tent, which was filled with horses. They arrived at the first stall just in time to see a tiny hoof descend from a heavily pregnant mare.

Lady Tabitha's mouth fell open and she froze in place. "Is she giving *birth*? Right here?"

"Before our very eyes," Hudson confirmed. "Behold, the miracle of life."

She clutched his arm as, inch by inch, a spindly foal dropped from his mother's womb to the packed brown dirt below.

Without taking even a moment's rest, the mother dipped her muzzle to her exhausted child, spending several long minutes cleaning him before beginning to nudge him urgently with her muzzle.

"Surely she cannot expect a newborn foal to—" Lady Tabitha gasped in awe. "He's *standing*. Already! It's scarcely been half an hour!"

Hudson could have watched Lady Tabitha watching the farm animals all week. He loved her genuine amazement, and the pleasure she took in simple moments that men like her father or Hudson's employer would consider common and vulgar. Life *was* wonderful, and a gift. Simple pleasures were often the best ones.

It was another quarter hour before Lady Tabitha could pull herself away from the newborn foal and venture on to the next tent.

The moment she and Hudson stepped inside, they were immediately accosted by a harried matron in a white apron.

"Oh, thank God," the woman said, pulling Lady Tabitha forward. "The competition was supposed to start an hour ago, and the judge never arrived. You'll do."

"But... I..." Lady Tabitha looked over her shoulder helplessly at Hudson, who hurried to catch up.

"Sit here," the matron commanded, pointing Lady Tabitha toward a pair of empty wooden chairs. "You too, sir."

"I'm not a sir," Hudson murmured.

"Well, you're a judge for the next ten minutes. The children have waited long enough."

Bemused, he took his seat beside Lady Tabitha as a sextet of little boys and girls no older than nine or ten years old marched proudly into view, each bearing a fifteen-pound creature clutched in their arms.

Lady Tabitha stared. "Are those... badgers?"

"They are, indeed," Hudson confirmed. The creatures' distinct black-and-white striped faces, gray fur, and short fluffy tails were unmistakable.

"How am I supposed to pick the best one?" she whispered.

"Eenie, meenie, miney, moe?" he whispered back.

"Do you know much about badgers?"

"Not a blessed thing," he answered cheerfully. "But all of these specimens look quite badger-y to me."

"We can do this." Lady Tabitha straightened, and addressed each child in turn. "Please tell me about your pet."

The children were eager to comply, full of proud smiles and long stories about how each creature got its name, as well as what it ate, and what its sleeping habits were like.

When they finished, Lady Tabitha looked anguished rather than illuminated.

"I can't pick just one," she muttered.

"You have to," the matron said firmly. "That's what a competition *is*."

Lady Tabitha bit her lip, then brightened. "All right. I've got it."

All six hopeful children stared at her expectantly.

"In keeping with centuries of Marrywell tradition…" Lady Tabitha pointed at each badger in turn. "That one is the May Day badger king, that one is the May Day badger queen, and the other four are the May Day badgers fair."

"That's not how it work—" the matron began.

It was too late. The children were squealing with joy, delighted at all the badgers having won prestigious titles. Before the aproned matron could interrupt further, the children ran off in all directions to brag to their parents and show off their newly crowned royal badgers to anyone who would listen.

Hudson grinned at Lady Tabitha. "That was very well done."

She let out an exhausted sigh and rested her temple briefly on his shoulder. "I was terrified for a moment there."

"You were perfect." He fought the urge to kiss the top of her head. She was not his, no matter how much he wished otherwise.

She straightened and gave him a shy smile. "I'm having more fun with you than I've ever had before in my life. I'm *glad* we ended up here together."

His heart warmed and his skin flushed. He wished he could promise to give her a lifetime of happiness. "Do you know what you need?"

"Please don't suggest livestock of my own," she moaned.

He pulled her to her feet. "How does a lemon ice sound?"

"Like a life saver," she said fervently, and took his arm with a smile. "Lead the way."

CHAPTER 6

"Who's the chit with the crown?" Mr. Frampton asked later that evening.

"May Queen," Tabitha answered. "It's the very highest honor to be so crowned."

"Ah. Like the badgers." He paused. "Why aren't you the May Queen?"

"I'm ineligible."

"Ineligible!" He reared back to stare at her. "You must be one of the most eligible young ladies here. Intelligent, beautiful, the daughter of a marquess—"

A blush heated her cheeks. "Not ineligible in that way. The May Queen and King are always the pair considered the most successful love match made during the festivities the year before. I was betrothed long before I attended my first May Day festival."

And they both knew hers was no love match.

Mr. Frampton considered her. "You've never been courted before."

She stared at him in confusion. "Viscount Oldfield—"

"—has been betrothed to you since you were a fetus. That's not courtship. That's a foregone conclusion. You've never had a true suitor?"

"How could I if, like you said, I've been promised elsewhere since birth?"

Mr. Frampton looked appalled. "Not even a stolen kiss?"

Of all the impertinent... She slid her hand from his elbow and crossed her arms. "Who I do and do not kiss is *my* business, not yours."

"That's a 'no'," he said. "Are the men in your life all corkbrains or cowards?"

"Perhaps too wise to risk the wrath of a viscount *and* a marquess," she reminded him. "You wouldn't have tried to steal a kiss either."

Mr. Frampton waggled his brows. "Would you like me to?"

She swatted at him. "It's not stealing a kiss if the woman *invites* you to."

But now that he'd put the idea into her head... Yes. Yes, she might like Mr. Frampton to steal a kiss. The thought of never experiencing anything but the press of her lips against the viscount's cadaver teeth was suddenly more than Lady Tabitha could bear.

Like everything else, she would have to bear it anyway. She rolled back her shoulders. Stiff upper lip. She was a marquess's daughter. Tabitha had never willingly disappointed her father. She definitely would not do so on his deathbed.

"Lady Tabitha!" squealed a familiar voice. It was Nancy Pringle. "Come join us!"

"Please give me a moment," she murmured to

Mr. Frampton. "I'm going to greet a few old friends."

He inclined his head and dropped back a few feet to give her space.

"Tabitha!" Miss Pringle threw a tipsy arm around her shoulders. "Do you see who I see?"

"Good gracious, how much ratafia have you drunk?" Tabitha tried to peel her friend's heavy arm from her shoulders.

Miss Pringle pointed across the crowd. "See that man? He's a French prince. Or a prince from some French-speaking country, I cannot remember. I'm going to marry him and become a princess. Can you introduce me?"

Tabitha pushed down Miss Pringle's pointing finger, then followed the direction of her gaze. An unknown, exceptionally tall man dressed in impeccable French fashions strolled alongside... a disheveled and unshaven Duke of Southbury?

No, it couldn't be. The Duke of Southbury famously did not pursue romantic entanglements, or allow a single hair of his ducal head to break free of sartorial perfection. He certainly wouldn't be at a matchmaking festival looking like he'd just woken up from a full week of carousing.

"That's no one," she told Miss Pringle firmly. "Why don't we find a booth selling nice hot cups of tea, and you can—"

"How many times must I shoo you back to your pen, little piglet?" came a loud voice just behind them.

Tabitha whirled to see Miss Bernice Charlton bearing down on Miss Matilda Dodd, a sweet country girl Tabitha had befriended. She clenched her fists. Bernice had been proclaimed the "diamond" of the ton two years running, and never let the other unwed ladies forget it. Apparently, the diamond felt compelled to exert her dominance over rural young women as well.

"Bernice, stop it." Tabitha reached her side in two strides. "Haven't you a cauldron to go and stir?"

Bernice glared at Tabitha. "Well, if it isn't the future viscountess. I suppose you think you're better than all the rest of us, because you've got a title on the hook."

"I don't think I'm better than any—"

"For your information, *I* will soon have a title on the hook as well. This little piglet's guardian is none other than the Earl of Gilbourne. Who is here shepherding our little piglet, which makes him ripe for the plucking," Bernice finished in satisfaction.

"I... don't even know how to untangle that mixed metaphor," Tabitha said. "If you think you can enamor the earl, go and try your best, but leave poor Miss Dodd out of it."

Bernice harrumphed and flounced off, her entourage trailing her like pastel ducklings.

"Thank you for saving me yet again," said Miss Dodd, then glanced over Tabitha's shoulder and frowned. "Look, an older gentleman is heading this way. Isn't that—"

"No," Tabitha groaned, and slowly turned around. "Please tell me it's not my intended."

It was.

Viscount Oldfield had arrived at the festival— and had been here for who knew how long. He was also flagrantly peering down the bodices of every young woman within eyesight. None of whom was his future bride.

They were debutantes. Five or more years younger than Tabitha.

"*Must* you marry him?" Miss Dodd asked with obvious repugnance.

"Unfortunately, yes. I cannot remember a time when I didn't know I was betrothed to Lord Old-field," Tabitha answered. "When I was young, it didn't seem real. Part of me thought I could still have a normal come-out with suitors, flowers, and a chance to fall in love. But that's not my lot. Yes, I must marry him. I have no choice."

Miss Dodd shook her head. "There's always choices. Look at him, making choices left and right. My advice? If you want to fall in love before you get married, do it."

Tabitha gave a sad chuckle. "If only it were so easy. No gentleman will come near me. The viscount comports himself exactly as you see before you, but when it comes to me... He's let it be known that I am his property. The lack of vows don't matter, because he's staked his claim."

"Then just be so awful that he won't want you," Miss Dodd suggested. "That's what I do with the earl. It's working for me."

Tabitha raised her brows. "*Is* it working?"

She'd seen the way the Earl of Gilbourne gazed at Miss Dodd when he thought she wasn't looking.

Miss Dodd's cheeks flushed pink. "All right, maybe it's more complicated than that."

"I wish life wasn't complicated at all," Tabitha said with feeling.

Her most fervent dream was to be released from this arranged marriage to a man she could not stand—and who patently had only the most superficial interest in her.

Tabitha wanted to be chosen for *herself*. Not for her age or her bosom or for the sake of convenience. She didn't want to be a pawn in a lordly chess match. Or a consolation prize to a viscount who found her interchangeable with any other.

She dreamed of a love match. A real one. Birds and flowers and butterflies.

But even the best dreams came to an end.

"My father has no male heirs," Tabitha said softly. "The marquessate dies with him because I was born the wrong gender. Papa's sole legacy is for me to make a match that unites our bloodline with the Medfords. One little ceremony will heal a generations-old rift. And even if that weren't the case, the damage is done. I'm already promised. Viscount Oldfield is my father's bosom friend and… a fine catch." She choked on the words. "If granting the dying wish of a father I adore is within my power, I must do it."

Even if it killed her in the process.

CHAPTER 7

After the arrival of Lord Oldfield in Marrywell, the festival became significantly less enjoyable. Tabitha mourned the loss of her earlier pleasant days exploring the village and attending events alongside Mr. Frampton, but he could no longer even speak to her with his employer present. With the atmosphere thus spoilt, Tabitha made no objection to traveling home to London early.

In truth, she also missed her father. Every time she was away from him, she feared he would no longer be there when she returned. That day was imminent. But knowing the fate that awaited him did not make Tabitha feel any more prepared for his loss.

Hours later, she knelt once again by his bedside. This time, they were alone, save for a discreet footman and the omnipresent physician.

"Are you certain I should attend more balls, Papa? I don't mind staying in with you."

"Of course you should go," he rasped. "We both know you won't attend a thing during your year of mourning. I'd prefer you to make the most of your life while I still have mine to see it happen."

Tabitha swallowed hard. The reminder of his impending demise was unnecessary and unwelcome. But the point of his message remained sound.

She nodded and squeezed his hand. "I just fear—"

The marquess turned his head. "Doctor, tell her what you told me this morning."

Dr. Collins spoke briskly. "Your father's health, while fragile, appears to be stable. You might have as much as two more months left together."

Might. As if two months were a long time.

Then again, maybe they were. If Papa had eight weeks left, there was no reason to rush into a marriage with Viscount Oldfield. The nuptials could take place next month, and there would still be plenty of time.

Tabitha opened her mouth to make her case.

Before she could do so, a coughing fit overtook her father. Dr. Collins rushed over to help, while Tabitha looked on, concerned.

At last, the coughing subsided. Her father sent her a weary look. "Go and enjoy your youth, daughter. We'll talk later."

Tabitha squeezed his hand. She hated to leave him like this. But he needed his rest far more than she needed to pester him by pleading for a postponement to her wedding. So she kissed his clammy forehead and trudged back to her bedchamber, where Mary Frances eagerly waited to prepare her mistress for tonight's ball.

Perhaps a change of scenery was just what Lady Tabitha needed.

By the time she alighted from the carriage, Tabitha was in much better spirits.

That was, until Lord Oldfield stepped out of the carriage behind hers.

It was all Tabitha could do not to groan in frustration. She hadn't been able to avoid the viscount in Marrywell, and now the same would be true back home in London.

After a perfunctory greeting, however, the viscount seemed content to ignore his betrothed and flit through the ballroom to peer down bodices, wine in one hand and a quizzing glass in the other.

Instead of accompanied by her betrothed, Tabitha found herself flanked by dual chaperones: her lady's maid, and Mr. Frampton.

"What are you doing here?" she asked the latter with surprise. "Shouldn't a man of business have… well, *business* to deal with?"

"Apparently, you *are* my business." His dark brown eyes were warm, and his low voice as rich as fine chocolate. "I'm not to let you out of my sight until you become Viscountess Oldfield."

"And *then* you need no longer worry about me?" she said in confusion. What could it mean? Perhaps the answer was as old as time.

For years, she had thought Lord Oldfield's interest in her was because she was female and young. Whilst he clearly still held that preference, perhaps the advantage to marrying Tabitha was about more than mere access to her body. The viscount didn't seem particularly mawkish about healing the rift between the two families.

Which might mean, what he really wanted was… her dowry. Ever since her come-out, when she'd first glimpsed his behavior toward the other debutantes, Tabitha had wondered if money had been Lord Oldfield's true game all along.

As the only child, Tabitha was the sole heir to her father's vast wealth. The title might expire along with the marquess, but his riches went along with his daughter. And since wives could not own property… that meant every penny of it would soon belong to Viscount Oldfield.

No wonder he had gone along with their ridiculous betrothal. The "match" might even have been the viscount's idea. Papa was softhearted enough to sacrifice his daughter for the wellbeing of two powerful families. And Lord Oldfield was self-serving enough to take advantage of the situation for his own ends.

What would happen to Tabitha after the wedding? Would she be free to live her life as she saw fit, or would she be shuttered away from society whilst her husband frolicked through the rest of his life spending every shilling of her father's money?

"Oh, dear," murmured Mr. Frampton. "It appears you've come to much the same conclusions I have."

She grimaced. "I'm feeling the weight of it."

Her shoulders slumped. Going to Papa with her suspicions would not change anything. Of course Lord Oldfield would gain control of Tabitha's life and finances. But she wasn't being singled out as a martyr. That was how marriage worked for everyone.

She was just foolish enough to have dreamt it might play out in a love match, rather than… like this.

Her old friend Lord Carnaby materialized before her with a smile. "A new set is starting. Dare I hope I might claim this dance?"

"My pleasure." Out of reflex, Tabitha placed her fingers on his palm and allowed him to lead her onto the parquet.

The truth was, it wasn't her pleasure. She'd rather have stayed with Mr. Frampton. No—she'd rather have *danced* with Mr. Frampton. Her heart thumped at the idea. Good heavens, she wasn't becoming soft on her bodyguard, was she?

Though if she were, who could blame her? He was not only the handsomest man in the ballroom, but also the one person who understood what was happening in her life.

He saw her clearly, as well as everything around them. That clear-eyed gaze could be disconcerting, but it was also a comfort. With him, she needn't be Lady Tabitha, proper, demure, and dutiful young lady.

With him, she could simply *be*. She hadn't realized how freeing that sensation could be.

For the next twenty minutes, however, her conversational partner was Lord Carnaby—and their only topics apparently the state of the weather, the quality of the music, and what a successful crush tonight was turning out to be.

The same exact conversation Tabitha had politely, demurely, and dutifully endured during every other dance with every other partner.

Somehow, she suspected Mr. Frampton would have something more interesting to say.

After the set ended, Lord Carnaby started to return her to her maid. Tabitha caught sight of her betrothed's nephew and heir presumptive, Reuben Medford, also exiting the dance floor with his wife.

"Thank you, Lord Carnaby," she murmured. "I see someone I must speak to."

Tabitha wasn't actually certain she had ever been properly introduced to Mr. Medford, though his reputation certainly preceded him. For years, he had been as much a rakehell as his uncle had been a shameless roué.

Until he met his wife.

Mr. Medford was now visibly, blissfully, happily married. He never so much as glanced at other women. Even after a full year of marriage, his besotted gaze never left his wife's shining face. It was everything a romantic heart like Tabitha's had ever dreamed of.

She decided to approach them before she lost her nerve. If Tabitha was to marry Mr. Medford's uncle in order to settle the longstanding feud between their two families, then perhaps it was past time to discover for herself what that side of the family was like.

And whether they were worth it.

CHAPTER 8

*V*iscount Oldfield's nephew Reuben Medford both did and did not look like a man who had once been an infamous rakehell. On the one hand, he was impeccably tailored: a man who did not need a mirror to know he was one of the most well put-together gentlemen in the ballroom. On the other hand, Mr. Medford did not appear cognizant of the many admiring glances sent his way. One hundred percent of his attention was centered wholly on his wife.

Gladys Medford, for her part, was also an intriguing figure. She was not classically beautiful—if anything, her features and coloring should not have added up to anything better than merely "plain"—yet her graceful bearing and the confidence that exuded from every inch of her made her seem much larger than her diminutive size, and so beautiful she dazzled.

Tabitha approached with caution. She arrived almost within arm's reach of the besotted couple before their gazes broke from each other to notice the interloper in their midst.

"Forgive me for approaching without a proper introduction," Tabitha began. "I'm—"

"Lady Tabitha," Mr. Medford finished with a welcoming grin. "Forgive *me* for not having orchestrated an introduction long before now."

She stared at him. "Why would you have done?"

"For starters, because my father—may he rest in peace—forbade me from having any contact with your family. Which of course made an adolescent boy absolutely wild to make your acquaintance."

"Then why didn't you do so?" asked his wife.

"I was a budding rakehell," he explained. "And Lady Tabitha seemed like a good girl. I didn't wish to ruin her reputation by association."

"You had no such compunction with me," Mrs. Medford teased.

"I didn't know you were you," her husband protested. "Had I known…"

"You wouldn't have compromised me?" she guessed dryly.

He kissed her cheek. "I would've presented myself to your father the very next morning."

"Humph." Mrs. Medford turned to Tabitha. "I hope you're courted by a man who shows up when he says he will."

"I'm not courted by anyone," said Tabitha.

Mrs. Medford's face showed her confusion. "Why on earth not? Have you some delightfully dreadful habit not currently visible to my eyes?"

"She has something dreadful, all right," said Mr. Medford. "She's betrothed to my uncle."

Mrs. Medford gasped. "Not *this* young lady!

You poor dear." Her face flushed. "That is… er… Does this moment call for congratulations or condolences?"

Tabitha grinned despite herself. "A little of both, probably. I am disappointed not to have been given an opportunity to make a love match, but I am honored to know my impending marriage to the viscount will unite both our families and put paid to generations of acrimony."

Mr. Medford paused. "Um… Will it?"

"Er… Won't it?" It was Tabitha's turn to be confused.

He made a face. "It's just… When I was instructed never to speak to you, you by definition already existed, which means you were already betrothed to my uncle. If your union were to resolve all wounds, wouldn't it have started then?"

"A betrothal is words, not action." Tabitha wasn't surprised a promise made before she was born hadn't immediately ameliorated the bad blood between the two families. Both sides would be waiting to see what the other chose to *do* about it.

Mrs. Redford rapped her husband's lapel with the back of her fingers. "Didn't you tell me your father and grandfather were impossible to please? Besides, they're gone, and have been for two years. The important part is the family you both have left."

"All I have left is my father," Tabitha said quietly. "And not for long."

"And all I have left is my uncle," said Mr. Medford. "Which is why I'm heir apparent to the viscountcy. Unless you give uncle some sons, of course. I'll be honest: I won't mind not inheriting. I like my life quite as it is."

Tabitha was barely attending to his words. Her brain was stuck back on each of them only having one family member left. Relatives who, by all appearances, *already* got along like two peas in a pod. If there was no one left who was keeping the grudge alive, then was her sacrifice necessary at all?

"Forgive my husband for prattling on," said Mrs. Medford. "Did you just want to meet us, or is there something we could help you with?"

"I don't know," Tabitha stammered. "I had also been warned about the Medford family as a child. Unlike yours, my father told me it was my sacred duty to unite the two clans. I thought I ought to meet your side, to see if it seemed worth…"

"Marrying Oldfield?" Mr. Medford said dryly.

"Worth attempting to heal the rift," Tabitha hedged.

"Consider it healed." Mr. Medford grabbed her hand and shook it. "See that? You mended fences with a simple conversation. When possible, I always advise befriending people with words, rather than by marrying their horrid uncle."

"I have to say, I agree," said Mrs. Medford. "Don't sacrifice your own future to solve someone else's problem. Parents who don't care about their children's happiness aren't worth the heartache they cause. I would know."

Tabitha believed her. But Mrs. Medford's relationship with her parents—or lack thereof—had little to do with Tabitha's. If one of the reasons behind the union was no longer as valid as it had been back when the betrothal had originally been minted, well… It didn't change anything important.

Her father wanted her to be respectable. He wanted her to marry his best friend, who was also a lord, and therefore the sort of catch matchmaking mamas dreamed of. She would have the protection of her husband's wealth and rank.

Most importantly, this marriage was her beloved father's dying wish.

"I hate to tell you this," said Mr. Medford, "but here comes Uncle now."

Tabitha jerked her startled gaze over her shoulder in time to see her betrothed exit the gaming room with a perturbed expression on his florid face. He glanced about the ballroom without peering down bodices for once, using his quizzing glass until his enlarged eye fell upon Tabitha.

The viscount strode in their direction with vigor.

"*There* you are," he hissed when he reached Tabitha's side.

"She certainly wasn't in the gaming room," Mr. Medford agreed.

Lord Oldfield ignored his nephew, opting instead to grasp Tabitha's wrist. "Waiting for banns is a stupid idea. We should make our union official while you're still young and attractive."

Mr. Medford looked mystified. "How much older and uglier can anyone be in three weeks' time?"

"It doesn't matter," the viscount snapped. "There's no sense wasting time courting a chit I'm

already betrothed to. My man of business has procured a special license. I shan't wait any longer."

"But there's less than two weeks left," Tabitha
protested. "And Father promised it was all right to
wait."

"I don't care what your father said. That was
before." The viscount's grip tightened around
Tabitha's wrist. "Remember, you're marrying *me*.
First thing tomorrow morning. You promised to
obey."

Tabitha's blood flooded with panic. "But—"

"I'll inform the marquess of the change in
plans. He'll be relieved. And he'll be alive to see his
promise fulfilled." Lord Oldfield's eyes glittered. "I
can't wait for our private celebration tomorrow
night."

CHAPTER 9

The next morning, Hudson stood at the altar in the front of the church as though he were a nervous groom awaiting his bride. But Lady Tabitha was not to be his wife, and this was not Hudson's wedding. His stomach roiled in protest.

The bride belonged to Lord Oldfield—who was conspicuously absent. Hudson had bundled him into the carriage and brought him here, only for the viscount to wander off to... who even knew? Hudson would have followed, had he not been instructed to keep a watchful eye on the future viscountess instead.

Obviously, Hudson wasn't allowed anywhere near the ladies' retiring room. Not that Lady Tabitha was currently sequestered in there, awaiting her cue as was customary. For better or worse—depending how superstitious you were— the bride was already here in the chapel, less than an arm's width away from her ailing father, the Marquess of Brigsby.

Lord Brigsby was in a special chaise longue

with iron wheels and a padded seat for comfort. Despite the bespoke craftsmanship, he didn't look the slightest bit comfortable. His face was pallid and gray, and his shoulders and spine hunched alarmingly, when not wracked by violent coughs.

According to the attending physician, Dr. Collins, the Marquess of Brigsby was still holding steady. Another month at least before there was reason to fear an imminent demise. Nonetheless, it was perhaps not the worst idea for Viscount Oldfield to insist on moving up the ceremony, just in case.

Not that Oldfield was particularly concerned about the marquess's diminishing health. There was a time-sensitive investment opportunity on the horizon. One the viscount could only take advantage of if Lady Tabitha's dowry was deposited into his account before the week's end.

Even if the Marquess of Brigsby had been in the pink of health, Lord Oldfield would still have gathered everyone in this chapel before the investment opportunity vanished. Hudson wanted to shake the man until he realized the true worth of the bride right before his eyes.

Lady Tabitha looked… distraught. And beautiful. A proper gothic heroine. Forced to wed a man she did not love because it was the dying wish of the father she *did* love.

For the rushed ceremony, Hudson had only himself to blame. Curse his thoroughness and efficiency! Oldfield wouldn't even *know* about the investment opportunity if Hudson hadn't been so good at his job.

His gaze settled back on Lady Tabitha, deep in

conversation with her father. She wore a gorgeous satin gown of deep rose, with a scooped bodice and charming puffed sleeves. Hudson didn't recognize the dress. He wondered if she'd had it made for the occasion, or if it was something she had worn to countless soirées and dinner parties. He had seen this coiffure before. It always looked touchably soft. God help him, everything about her always looked touchably soft.

Hudson spent far too much time thinking about Lady Tabitha.

They were only six years apart, but an entire world stretched between them. Ironic that a viscount a generation and a half her senior made a "good" match, whereas the mere idea of Lady Tabitha casting her gaze at a man closer to her age but beneath her station would have had everyone in the room objecting.

Not that there were many people in the room. Hudson and Lady Tabitha. Her father, and his physician. A footman for the wheeled chair. The bride's lady's maid, Mary Frances. The priest. All in all, a sparse turnout for an allegedly happy occasion.

None of the witnesses were smiling. One would be forgiven for thinking they'd come to a funeral, not a wedding. Even the priest looked stoic.

Lady Tabitha glanced over her shoulder in Hudson's direction. He froze, his gaze caught in hers. Her pale face looked terrified, but determined. She murmured something to her father, then plodded up the aisle to join Hudson at the altar.

"Any idea where my groom is?" she asked quietly.

"He's here," Hudson assured her.

The viscount was definitely… somewhere. If this was a ballroom, Hudson's money would be on a gaming room of some type. But this was a church. Perhaps Lord Oldfield was off sampling the communion wine.

Lady Tabitha herself looked as though a slug or two of brandy wouldn't go amiss. In fact, she looked as though she were one loud noise away from turning on her heels and fleeing the chapel altogether. Hudson's heart ached for her. He wished he could throw her over his shoulder and escape into the sunset with her, never to be heard from again.

Such a silly thought. He would never get to touch her at all, much less manhandle her like a sack of potatoes. Theirs was not a romance, no matter what Hudson's private thoughts might wish. For the past decade, he'd watched her from afar and pined desperately. And for a few days in Marrywell, he spent an unprecedented amount of time with Lady Tabitha… falling even harder for her than before. All of which was good practice for the upcoming decades of watching after her from under the same roof.

Minus the pining. Once she spoke her vows to his employer, Hudson would not entertain lustful thoughts about another man's wife. Or at least try not to. He would protect her with his life, and nothing more.

Which meant he was down to scant minutes

left to cram in all the last remaining lustful thoughts he could think.

"Perhaps it won't be as bad as you fear," he murmured.

Her startled gaze snapped to his. "You think I fear this marriage?"

"You look like you want to vomit," he admitted.

"I do want to vomit." She made a face. "I just hoped it didn't show."

"I'm not certain anyone else has noticed," he offered.

"Except for you, the man who notices everything?"

Everything about her, anyway. "Jitters are normal. Is there anything I can do to help?"

"Take Oldfield's place?" she muttered.

Hudson's heart stopped, then fluttered against his rib cage. "What did you just say?"

"Nothing. Of course I'll marry the man my father has chosen for me. Betrothal is a time-honored tradition that stretches back for centuries. Only a fool would lament the loss of a love match that never existed."

The entire practice made Hudson livid. "Grieving a loss is never foolish."

"What about attending a matchmaking festival when I'm already betrothed? *That's* foolish."

He shook his head. "Being somewhere that makes you happy is always time well spent."

"What about pledging myself to someone who has no wish to make me happy?"

Hudson closed his mouth.

Her lips pursed with self-deprecation. "You can't answer that without losing your post, so I'll answer for both of us. Willfully sublimating my own peace and joy in the name of fulfilling someone else's desires is—"

"*Noble*," he said firmly. At least, Hudson hoped it was.

As the viscount's employee, Hudson put his own wishes at a distant second every minute of every day. He would not have wished such a fractured life onto anyone, much less Lady Tabitha, but Hudson had been in earnest when he'd said respecting her father was a noble path.

Noble and sad. A waste of a life. All to honor a longstanding tradition of betrothing children to strangers without the least attempt to ask them what they want or give them what they need.

The rear door to the sanctuary opened and Lord Oldfield walked in at last. His cravat was askew. Hudson hoped the viscount hadn't been out in the alley tupping a prostitute instead of standing at the altar awaiting his bride.

"The wait is over," he murmured. "The ceremony can begin."

Lady Tabitha clutched her stomach as though she really might vomit all over her pretty pink dress.

Lord Oldfield strode up to them, then turned to bark at the priest, "Well? I haven't all day. I'm a busy man. Can't you make this fast?"

The priest looked startled, but cleared his throat and began the opening speech.

"Why are you still standing up here with us?" the viscount snapped at Hudson.

"My apologies." The back of Hudson's neck burned. Now that the viscount was here and the ceremony underway, Hudson's presence was no longer necessary at the altar. This wasn't his wedding. He stepped into the aisle to return to the pews.

Lady Tabitha grabbed his arm.

He placed his hand over hers out of instinct.

"I can't do this," she whispered. "Not yet. It's too fast."

"Good God, don't cling at my servants," said Lord Oldfield in obvious affront. "I expect my wife to show proper decorum at all times. Mr. Frampton, unhand her at once so that she can marry *me*."

The priest had ceased speaking. Everyone else was staring.

Hudson dropped his hand from Lady Tabitha's.

"I need the retiring room." She bolted down the aisle and out the door, her lady's maid at her heels.

"Don't just stand there, Frampton," Oldfield snapped in exasperation. "Go and *fetch* her."

"From the ladies' retiring room?" Hudson asked pointedly. "What happened to decorum at all times?"

"Well, stand outside the door, at least, and bring her back here the moment she exits."

Hudson inclined his head and set off down the aisle, pausing only to glance down at Lord Brigsby as he passed.

"You think my daughter is all right?" the marquess rasped.

No, Hudson did not think Lady Tabitha was all right. She was being used like a pawn by both of the men who ought to be protecting her. But Hudson could not say that and keep his post.

Which was the only way for Hudson to keep watch over Lady Tabitha.

"She wishes to make you proud," he hedged instead.

"I'm already proud," said the marquess. "Seeing my girl wed will be the happiest moment of my life."

Even though it would be the worst moment of hers…

Or the first of many.

CHAPTER 10

*T*abitha barely made it to the retiring room before hunching over, hands on her knees, to gasp for air. The floor and ceiling seemed to tilt around her as she fought to catch her breath.

Her disequilibrium had begun in the chapel. What had started as a large, pretty, mostly empty room had slowly pressed closer and closer around her, squeezing out all the oxygen until all that was left was her pounding heart and a pinprick of light on the other side of the far door.

Tabitha had instinctively made a run for it before even that narrow avenue of escape disappeared, too.

The door swung open behind her. She spun, expecting to find the concerned eyes of Mr. Frampton—or worse, the miffed annoyance of her soon-to-be husband. Never mind that part of her panic had set in when he'd kept her waiting, when he should have been there first all along.

The interruption was neither of the men, but rather, her lady's maid, Mary Frances.

Tabitha sagged with relief and slumped down onto a short, padded wooden stool.

Her maid approached cautiously. "They're all waiting for you."

"I know."

"Your exit made quite a scene."

"*I know.*"

"Are you going to go back in there?"

Was there any other option? And yet… Tabitha dropped her face into her hands. "I don't know."

After a long pause, Mary Frances spoke again. "Do you want me to freshen your hair?"

Tabitha glanced up. "Did my mad dash ruin my coiffure?"

"Your ringlets might have become a bit… asymmetrical."

Tabitha craned her neck until she could catch sight of herself in the looking-glass and let out a choking sound. A bit asymmetrical? She looked as though the walls really had closed in on her, and she'd been forced to pull these ringlets out from the rubble.

"I look a proper mess," she admitted. "Might as well get married that way."

Mary Frances bit her lip, then gestured toward a leather bag in the corner. "All our things are still in here, if you change your mind. There's no fire for the curling tongs, but I brought a variety of pins and hair combs."

Of course she did. Mary Frances always thought of everything. She was like Mr. Frampton in female form.

If only she could think of a way to extricate Tabitha honorably from this cursed matrimony.

A heavy fist pounded on the door. "Lady Tabitha?"

Ah. There was Mr. Frampton, as anticipated. Of course Tabitha's future husband would send a lackey rather than check on his bride-to-be himself.

The knocking grew louder. "Lady Tabitha? Are you all right?"

"I'm fine!" she shouted, then whispered to Mary Frances, "Please lock the door."

Mary Frances hurried to do as she'd been asked.

"You didn't look fine," Mr. Frampton called through the door. "Can I fetch you a cup of tea? Or a shot of brandy?"

Tabitha leaned her head back against the wall and closed her eyes to block out his words. Mr. Frampton had turned out to be so *nice*, damn him. His unflagging empathy made the contrast between him and his employer all the more stark. Oh, why couldn't her father have betrothed her to the sort of man who cared about her well-being and offered to bring her brandy in church?

Not for the first time, she wished she were marrying Mr. Frampton rather than Viscount Oldfield.

A laughable fantasy. Mr. Frampton was her fiancé's foot soldier and loyal to a fault. He genuinely cared about Tabitha's well-being, she believed that to her core. But she also knew that the moment she emerged from this retiring room, no matter how tender Mr. Frampton's feelings toward her, he would drag her straight back to the altar so that she could become his employer's property.

"Perhaps brandy *in* the tea?" Mr. Frampton tried again.

"I'm fine!" she called out, trying to infuse her voice with pep and joviality. "Go back to the chapel. I'll be there in a minute."

"I'm not leaving you," he answered. "We can walk there together."

Tabitha's eyes met Mary Frances's.

"He's not leaving you," Mary Frances whispered.

"I heard him," Tabitha whispered back.

"He scares me," Mary Frances added.

"Scares you! Why on earth do you say that?"

"He's so… big and strong and intense. Every muscle always bunched and tense, as if primed for action. He watches everything, like a bird of prey, waiting for just the right moment to swoop in. Most of all, he watches you."

This description did not frighten Tabitha as much as Mary Frances might have predicted.

Yes, Mr. Frampton was big and strong and intense, but he was also sweet and handsome and kind. He had never once peered down her bodice with a quizzing glass or made her feel like a fruit ripe for the plucking. When Mr. Frampton looked Tabitha's way, it was with concern or genuine interest.

And duty. She could not forget the duty. No matter how kindhearted her bird of prey might be, he would still scoop her up and deposit her back in the viscount's nest as ordered.

The thought of sharing Lord Oldfield's bed

later tonight caused Tabitha's stomach to roil, and she doubled over, clutching both hands over her mouth.

"*Are* you all right?" Mary Frances asked, alarmed.

"As all right as I will ever be," Tabitha managed.

But the moment she stepped outside this room, she would not be all right ever again. Marriage to Lord Oldfield would be misery.

"I can't do it," she whispered.

Mary Frances's eyes widened. "You're going to *jilt* a viscount?"

Tabitha groaned. "No."

Much as she wanted to, she couldn't do that, either. Jilts were socially ruined, meaning Tabitha would *never* find an aristocratic husband.

Her only choices were Viscount Oldfield or nobody.

Between the two, she'd rather have nobody.

But there was her father to consider, and the promise she'd made him. He wasn't even strong enough to walk into the chapel on his own two feet. He certainly wasn't strong enough to withstand a daughter flinging his dying wish into his face because she didn't like the lord he'd chosen for her.

"I need more time," she muttered. "Time to think."

The knock came on the door again. "Lady Tabitha? Are you certain there's nothing I can bring you?"

"I'm fine," she shouted. "But this might take a while. Go back to the chapel."

"I'm not going anywhere until I see that you're

all right," he answered. "Take as much time as you need. I'll be here for you, when you're ready."

Tabitha grimaced and clenched her fists in her skirt. Those were the exact words she'd hungered for all this time… spoken by the man who could not give her what she needed.

If only Viscount Oldfield would let her take her time! If only her father would have let her make her own decisions!

"He's not going anywh—" Mary Frances began.

"I know. I knew as soon as he knocked that he wasn't going to leave." Tabitha rose carefully to her feet. "But perhaps I can."

Mary Frances frowned. "Return to the chapel, you mean? To finish the ceremony?"

That was definitely not what Tabitha meant. She hurried to a basin to splash some water on her face. "I'm taking the time I need. Or at least a sliver of it. Which means no wedding yet. Not to-day, anyway."

"I'm not sure that's true," Mary Frances said doubtfully. "Mr. Frampton will deliver you to the altar trussed like a pig if he has to."

And no one in the chapel would object to the ceremony continuing with the bride bound and gagged like a prisoner of war.

"Then I cannot allow Mr. Frampton to catch me," Tabitha said.

Mary Frances looked even less convinced of this notion. "I don't think he is the sort of man who… *fails*."

No. Tabitha didn't think so, either. She would have to move quickly.

"Change clothes with me," she said urgently.

Mary Frances's eyes widened in alarm. "What?"

"I need to wear something I can doff and don on my own. This gown is far too extravagant."

"But I'm here to help you with it," Mary Frances said with confusion. "I always help you with your clothing."

"You shan't for long," said Tabitha. "I'm going to escape out through the retiring room window. If you came with me, you'd be dismissed from your post."

"I'll be dismissed for letting you leave! Not that you can make it through that window. It's too small and five feet up."

"You shan't 'allow' me to leave. You couldn't if you wished to. I'm the mistress and you're the servant. Which means, you can't order me about. No matter how erratic my actions or ridiculous my commands, *your* orders are to follow them. Blame my escape on me. Tell them you tried everything you could."

Mary Frances bit her lip. "Where will you go?"

"I don't know. Somewhere. Anywhere."

Tabitha fumbled for the reticule in her hidden pocket. It didn't contain *all* her pin money—the sum wouldn't fit in such a small bag—but there was enough here to last for a year, if she were frugal. Not that she could be gone that long. She would never forgive herself if her father died whilst she was running away from her own future.

"Here." She handed Mary Frances a trio of gold guineas.

Her maid's jaw dropped with shock. "What's this for?"

"In case you do lose your post. I plan to be gone for at least a week."

"But this is more than I earn in a month!"

"And not nearly as much as you deserve. Leave an address behind if you are let go, and when I return, I'll make things right. Now, help me out of this gown and into yours."

Mary Frances sprang into action with alacrity. In no time, the two young women had exchanged dresses. Both looked decidedly uncomfortable in their new attire.

Before Tabitha could change her mind, she swung the stool beneath the window and climbed up.

"If you go out that window…" Mary Frances warned quietly.

Tabitha nodded with determination. "I know."

She would ruin her reputation. Cause a scandal. Annoy the viscount. Disappoint her father.

But she couldn't go through with the wedding. Not yet. If there was a second option, one in which she could make her father proud without marrying Lord Oldfield, then Tabitha needed time to think of it, and put those plans in motion.

She would not say her vows unless she meant them.

There had to be another way.

"Come closer," she whispered urgently. "I need to hoist myself on your shoulder to wiggle through the window."

Mary Frances approached dubiously. "If you rip that skirt, I haven't anything else you can wear."

Tabitha tamped down a hysterical laugh. She

was climbing out of a retiring room window to avoid her own wedding, and her lady's maid was worried about Tabitha looking bedraggled on the other side.

"I adore you, Mary Frances," Tabitha said as she hauled herself up and through the narrow window frame. "I'll see you in a week."

And with that, she dropped into freedom on the other side.

CHAPTER 11

*M*arrywell.

The quaint village had been the first place Tabitha had thought of when she'd ducked into a hackney carriage outside of the church. It was perfect for so many reasons. Marrywell was far enough away from London that nobody who had been at the church was likely to stumble across her. Despite being known as *the* place where people fell in love, this year's festival was now over. The streets and inns were empty, likewise ensuring Tabitha would have no problem staying out of sight.

Perhaps most importantly, Marrywell was somewhere Tabitha felt safe. A place where she'd been *happy*. For a woman with an unwanted marriage looming over her shoulders like a dark cloud, Tabitha was grateful for any scrap of joy she could find.

After checking into a different hotel than the one she usually booked—using "Mrs. Snowfeather" as a pseudonym—Tabitha cleaned up and went for a long walk in the botanical gardens to restore her battered spirit.

She might have postponed the wedding for the moment, but a battle still raged inside her.

On the one hand, she could not bear to become a lecherous old roué's possession and plaything. On the other hand, she had been raised to be a dutiful daughter. She *wanted* to please her father and make him proud.

Arranged and political marriages among the aristocracy was not a torture designed just for Tabitha, but an everyday occurrence no more remarkable than London rain. Who was she to think herself deserving of special circumstances?

By the time her stomach rumbled, Tabitha was no closer to making peace with her inescapable future. Because the matchmaking festival had concluded, the assembly rooms were closed, the brewer's field was empty, there were no activities on the stage or in the gardens. She would have plenty of time to be alone with her conflicting thoughts until she worked out what to do.

But first: supper. Tabitha glanced up and down the main street, then picked a public house at random. This one was called the Cork & Cupid. During the festival, the bustling interior had been packed to standing room only, but now, a fortnight after the fact, Tabitha was one of only a handful of guests inside the cozy wooden pub.

She took a table near a window and ordered the special of the day without even inquiring what it might be. She was not a picky eater. Tabitha was not a picky anything… save, apparently, for selecting a husband to whom she would be happy to vow to love and obey.

Oh, how lucky were all the women who had come to Marrywell before her and found glorious love matches! Tabitha was so envious of every one of them, she could barely see straight. She didn't want to be a viscountess. She needn't be Lady anything at all. She'd take a blacksmith with a kind smile, an organist with a fine sense of humor, a candlestick-maker with a love of good books.

Social status didn't matter half as much as meeting the sort of man who would ask how she was doing and actually care about the answer.

"Lady Tabitha?" came a low, gentle voice filled with obvious relief. "Are you all right?"

She glanced up from her plate of fresh fish in shock.

Mr. Frampton stood beside her table, looking much the same as he had back at the church ten hours earlier, if a bit more wrinkled and with a slight shadow of stubble along his jaw. In other words, big and strong and frightening…ly handsome. His perennial good looks were not what surprised her.

"How did you find me so fast?" she said in dismay.

She'd hoped to have at least a week to herself. She was incognito in Mary Frances's plain maid's clothing, and she was paying for her rooms herself, rather than charging the costs to her father's accounts.

Even if someone, somewhere, had recognized her—which Tabitha was certain they had not, given that hardly anyone was still in town at all—

London was an eight-hour drive from Marrywell. If some wayward gossip had dispatched a footman with the news the moment Tabitha alighted from her hackney, the missive would still not cross her father's door for another six hours, at the earliest.

Mr. Frampton slid into the seat opposite her with a rueful smile. "Fast? You missed me dashing about in a panic from the moment you turned up missing. I was terrified that something awful had… I'm unspeakably relieved to find you well. I would have come here sooner, had I not stopped to check a few likely venues in London first."

"Like where?"

His neck flushed slightly. "Your rooms, obviously—"

"You went into my *bedchamber*?"

"—and the homes of those I thought might harbor you."

"*Harbor* me?"

"Friends like Miss Matilda Dodd, and her guardian Lord Gilbourne. Or family members like Mr. Reuben Medford and his wife."

"He's not my family. He's Viscount Oldfield's family."

"And yet, I quite suspect Mr. Medford would have happily offered you sanctuary, had you asked it of him."

"But… how did you guess Marrywell, of all places?"

"Of all places," Mr. Frampton repeated quietly. "It was right here on this street, the last time I saw you smile."

She stared at him, unsure how she felt about being seen so clearly.

The corners of his eyes crinkled, and he gestured at her plate. "Eat. Your food is growing cold."

She set down her fork and knife. "I think I'm done."

"Are you?"

Her lips tightened. "Done running, you mean? At ease, for a moment. I'll return eventually. I promise. I just need… a week to myself before I can submit to Fate."

His warm brown eyes were sad. "I'm afraid I cannot offer you that week. I've been tasked with bringing you home posthaste."

"Home?" she repeated with bitterness. "Or to the altar, to wed your employer?"

"His home will soon be yours," Mr. Frampton replied with equanimity.

"I won't go," she said.

"You will." His eyes were sympathetic, but resolute. As if he, too, hated what he had come to do… but would not allow his personal feelings to interfere with his duty to his employer.

"You can't make me," she insisted with more confidence than she felt.

"I most certainly can. You don't weigh more than ten or eleven stone. I can toss you over my shoulder and stroll out the door without breaking a sweat."

She glanced at his shoulder. It *was* wide and muscular. She had noticed those features on several occasions.

"I'll scream," she warned him.

He shrugged. "I'll say you're a runaway servant. No one will stop me."

"I'll…" *Cry.*

The truth was, Mr. Frampton was right. He *could* throw her over his shoulder like a wet towel and force her into a carriage that would take her straight back to the very future she was trying her hardest to avoid.

"Come." He placed his big warm hand over her cold, clammy, smaller one. "We've a long drive ahead of us."

"He can't expect me to marry him at four o'clock in the morning," she blurted out.

Mr. Frampton shook his head. "On that, you can rest easy. The priest has rescheduled your nuptials for next Sunday."

"Then I *do* have a week?" A sense of relief washed over her so profound it took her breath away.

"Yes." His eyes smiled at her. "You'll have a full week."

"In that case, there's no sense rushing back, is there?"

"I was told—"

"You were ordered," she muttered.

"Very well. My orders are to bring you back at once."

"But nobody but *us* knows you've already found me," she insisted, her tone pleading. "It could take a week of searching."

He simply arched his brows. "I'm very good at my job."

"Couldn't you try to be a little… *less* good at it?" she burst out.

After all that she'd gone through—jilting her betrothed at the altar, escaping in her maid's clothes through a retiring room window—Tabitha hadn't come this far to have all hope snatched away now.

Mr. Frampton regarded her gravely, his brown eyes searching hers. "What is it that you want?"

"I want…" The backs of her eyes stung, and she had to blink rapidly to keep the emotion at bay.

She wanted her father to love her. To care about her happiness.

She wanted a husband who saw her as a person deserving of respect, with thoughts and dreams and needs of her own.

She wanted a love match.

And failing that… She wanted at least one night of love.

Maybe this was her chance.

"If you give me this week," she said quietly, "I will go back willingly."

He looked understandably wary. "A week to do what?"

"To be alone with my thoughts."

"I won't leave you alone," he said firmly.

Of course not. He had no reason to trust her to stay where he could find her, for one. And he was under strict orders.

"Mostly alone, then." As she gazed at him, inspiration struck. "You can be my husband."

He reared back, his face a comical mix of shock and confusion. "I can be your *what*?"

"Not my real husband," she said quickly. "My fake husband. For the week. As you pointed out, I don't look like Lady Tabitha. The crowds are gone. We're here anonymously. In fact, I registered at my inn as Mrs. Snowfeather. You can be Mr. Snowfeather."

"What the devil is a snowfeather?"

"Please consider it. You can't tell me you haven't dreamed of enjoying a moment to yourself away from your employer. Why not take that time here and now?" She gave him her most winning smile. "With me!"

CHAPTER 12

*H*udson stared at Lady Tabitha, his insides a mixture of horror and longing.

Agreeing to be Mr. Snowfeather for even a second was a ridiculous, ill-advised idea that he certainly would not be acting on. Hudson would be dismissed from his post, for one. And this was his *employer's* bride, for two.

Then again...

Lady Tabitha had made several sound points. Hudson was preternaturally good at his job, but no one *knew* he'd already found the runaway bride. By his own admission, her presence wasn't strictly necessary in London until the rescheduled wedding one week from today. She didn't want to go back until then. Her groom likewise held no intention of seeking her out until the ceremony— and possibly would arrive late for that as well, as he'd done this morning.

Though Lady Tabitha might find it difficult to imagine, Hudson empathized viscerally with the desire to get away, to start over, to have a different life, if only for a moment.

He had the luxury of determining his own future. Lady Tabitha did not. If she failed to make the most of the scant week that remained before her nuptials...

She would never have a second chance.

And neither would Hudson. He had dreamed of spending more time with her. As much as possible. More than was even allowed. Could he really bring himself to curtail their time together a minute sooner than absolutely necessary?

"Please?" she added sweetly, batting her eyelashes at him shamelessly.

Such transparent manipulation techniques would not work on Hudson. More importantly, Lady Tabitha didn't need them. His heart had softened for her years ago.

"I must return you to your future husband," he told her firmly.

"You will," she promised him. "One week from today."

He glanced over his shoulders. "Where is your maid?"

"I left Mary Frances at the chapel."

"I know, but... You don't have *any* chaperone?"

"How could I? I didn't want anyone to be dismissed from their post."

"Didn't want..." He groaned. "You need a keeper, Lady Tabitha."

She beamed at him. "*You* can be my keeper, Mr. Snowfeather. All week long."

"Stop calling me Mr. Snowfeather! I have not agreed to this scheme."

"Nor have you thrown me over your shoulder and marched off, as you threatened."

"And which is no doubt the wisest avenue."

"Why be wise?" she asked with surprising earnestness. "I have done everything I was supposed to do for twenty-two years. And what has it got me? A groom I don't want. Er, no offense."

Hudson shrugged. "I don't wish to marry him, either."

"But… aren't you supposed to convince me that *I* should want to?"

"Can anyone convince you of that?" Hudson leaned back in his seat. "Whether I like it or not, my job is to ensure you are at the chapel at nine o'clock in the morning next Sunday. What you reply when the priest asks you to make your vows is between you and God, not me."

"Then say yes," she begged. "All four of us will get what we want. Viscount Oldfield will have a willing bride, my father will witness the ceremony, I will have my first—and, likely, *only*—week of freedom in my life, and you…" Her smile fell. "…will be saddled with me for seven days. I'm sorry. You're the only one who won't get what you want."

That conclusion could not be further from the truth.

For years, Hudson had gone out of his way to have any spare second with Lady Tabitha that he could conjure. Drizzling? Why, Hudson happened to have an umbrella. A knot in your bonnet ribbon? Why, let me untie it for you. In need of an escort down the hall? Please, take my arm.

The two days he'd spent in her company at the

beginning of the matchmaking festival was the most time they'd shared together in their entire acquaintance… and it had been glorious. He'd lost track of the number of times they'd forgotten who they were and simply enjoyed each other's company like old friends.

Er, if one of the old "friends" pined after the other and yearned to pull her into his arms and kiss her.

An entire week alone with her was a dream come true. A dream he did not deserve. A dream he absolutely, positively, unquestionably should say no to, before things got even more out of hand.

Lady Tabitha's face fell, as though reading his thoughts.

"I just wanted… to be happy again. For a short while." Her expression was defeated. "It might be for the very last time."

Hudson's heart wrenched for her. From anyone else, that pronouncement might have sounded melodramatic. But Hudson had no reason to doubt his employer's proficiency in making everyone around him profoundly unhappy.

A bride would bear the worst of it. She would belong to the viscount, like a piece of art or an old shoe. And she'd have just as much autonomy.

That wasn't all, Hudson realized with a sinking feeling. Lady Tabitha might not even be referring to Lord Oldfield. Her father's imminent death had visibly weighed on her ever since the physician first pronounced him incurable. At any moment, Lady Tabitha would be plunged into a year of mourning, not just of her old life, but of her last remaining family member.

She was right. Things were about to get much worse.

What kind of beast would refuse to allow the fair maiden a short respite before the storm?

Hudson tightened his jaw and came to a decision. If he were going to have to hand over the woman of his dreams to a man who didn't deserve her, the least he could do was let her cross that bridge at her own pace.

"Six days," he said firmly. "We return to London no later than Saturday evening."

Lady Tabitha gasped, her brown eyes shimmering in relief. She scooped up his hands and brought his knuckles to her chest in gratitude. "Thank you. *Thank you*. You shan't regret this."

Regret this? Only a few seconds of their pact had transpired, and already Hudson's hands were nestled against the bosom of his employer's future bride.

It was definitely going to be a week to remember.

CHAPTER 13

*E*lation washed over Tabitha, accompanied by a bone-melting wave of relief. Mr. Frampton had found her, and he would return her, but not yet. She could still have her week of freedom.

Oh, very well: six days. Which were six more days of freedom than she would normally dream of. She would take them, and happily.

Tabitha was also glad Mr. Frampton was here with her. She'd enjoyed his company so much on their most recent visit to Marrywell, and had lamented being obligated to spend social outings with her own set instead of continuing her conversations with a man society considered beneath her.

She didn't think of him as beneath her at all. And now, he was right here next to her. Co-conspirators, who would forever have this secret—and a week full of memories—between them.

"You must be famished," Tabitha told him. "I can vouch for the special of the day."

His brows shot up. "Isn't it rude for a servant

to eat in front of a lady?"

"You're not a servant—you're an employee."

"Is there a difference?" he asked with amusement.

"You're not *my* employee, in any case. I can't help being a lady, but I *can* resolve any awkwardness of eating alone. Whilst you enjoy your supper, I shall indulge in cakes for dessert."

"I'll accept that deal." Mr. Frampton signaled the barmaid and placed the orders. As soon as the barmaid was gone, he returned his full focus back to Tabitha. "Now, as for the question of pretending to be your husband—"

"You agreed!"

"I agreed not to return you to *your* future husband until Saturday. That is stretching the rules enough without adding a Shakespearean farce to the mix."

"There's no reason to rent separate rooms when I've already got lodgings sorted."

"The reason is that you are an unwed young woman, alone in—"

"No one knows that. I've checked in as Mrs. Snowfeather. If you're worried about my reputation, cease at once. I've already spent several unchaperoned hours far from home. I'll be ruined if this much gets out. Pretending to be the King and Queen of France won't make it any worse."

"I rather think it might. It would be wisest to call the least attention to yourself as possible."

"In which case, renting separate rooms is out of the question," she replied with satisfaction. "Far more eyebrows will raise at a wayward wife, gallivanting around town with a handsome bachelor.

Yet it is utterly unremarkable for a married couple to spend time together."

He gazed at her for a long moment, his eyes unreadable. Then: "Handsome, am I?"

She blushed. "Tastes vary. I have mine."

His eyes glittered. "All the more reason not to tempt fate."

"Because otherwise we're fated to find ourselves in a compromising position?" she asked archly. "Such an objection would imply you find *me* attractive."

"I needn't 'imply' any such thing. Surely, you've glimpsed yourself in a looking-glass."

Her cheeks flushed hotter, but she didn't look away. "Tastes vary."

He inclined his head. "And I have mine."

She folded her hands together atop the table. "Would it help if I promise not to ravish you without your permission?"

His eyes heated, then cleared. "You'll find I am always in control of my actions."

"Then there can be no further objection. We are the completely un-scandalous Mr. and Mrs. Snowfeather for the rest of the week. It will be fun."

"It will be… something," he murmured.

The food arrived at that moment, curtailing the conversation.

As Tabitha nibbled at her cakes, she took the opportunity to regard Mr. Frampton from beneath her lashes.

Handsome? Such an inadequate word couldn't begin to explain his effect on her pulse… and her breathing… and her heart.

The only thing better than gazing upon him would be if she could reach out and touch the softness of his hair, the hardness of his muscles, the warmth of his skin, the rough tickle of his stubbled jaw against the sensitive pad of her thumb.

This thought was immediately followed by a stab of guilt. Not because of her intended husband. Tabitha had been betrothed to him against her will, and Viscount Oldfield certainly showed no inclination to hide his own lust for all the other young ladies and debutantes.

It was that she was so far from her father. She had never disappointed him before. Part of her longed to be at his side now, on her knees like a child, begging for him to understand. Another part of her knew that returning home for even a moment would curtail her newfound freedom forever. Father would never let her alone after this. Nor would Viscount Oldfield. If she returned to London now, it would be as a prisoner.

Nonetheless, she hated to think she was causing her father any pain. He was already dying. Tabitha did not want to add to his suffering.

Mr. Frampton's dark brown eyes locked on hers. "What is it?"

"What's what?"

"Something's wrong. Tell me, so that I can resolve it."

"You can't resolve it," she said bitterly.

He leaned back. "I can remedy anything. Ask Viscount Oldfield."

"You can't remedy my father's impending demise. Ask his physician, Mr. Collins."

"Ah." Mr. Frampton set down his fork. "You're afraid your father will pass whilst you are… How did you put it? Gallivanting around town with a handsome bachelor?"

She clenched her teeth at the flippant characterization, but nodded.

"I distinctly recall Dr. Collins clearly stating that your father has another month or two of life left in him."

"Even doctors can be wrong."

"You won't miss his last moments," Mr. Frampton said quietly. "Not this week. I'll handle it."

"How?"

"Like I handle everything. Trust me."

She *did* trust him, Tabitha realized. If anyone could make a ludicrous promise like, "Your father won't die without you at his bedside" and have it come true… that man was Mr. Frampton.

"All right." She took a deep breath. "I believe you. Thank you."

Three men burst through the door bearing lutes. They glanced around the empty public house, then bounded over to Tabitha and Mr. Frampton's table, beaming.

"Love birds!" they shouted, and launched into an energetic love ballad.

Mr. Frampton sent Tabitha a look of such absolute horror, it was all she could do not to dissolve into giggles.

Tabitha had heard of musicians serenading couples during the matchmaking festival. She hadn't expected it to happen to her and Mr. Frampton. Now that she thought about it, it didn't make sense that musicians like these would only work one week out of every year. They relied on vails for their income. A coin handed over directly after a serenade, or perhaps a passed hat if performing to a large gathering.

When the men finished their song, Tabitha reached for her reticule.

Mr. Frampton was faster. He placed a coin in each musician's palm, politely yet pointedly communicating that their continued performance was unnecessary.

The musicians glanced at the crowns in their hands with obvious surprise and clapped him on the shoulder jovially as they took their leave.

"That was kind of you," Tabitha said. "Particularly since you didn't want them here at all."

He shrugged. "They played well, and there's no one else here to give them a vail."

"Not just any vail. Three crowns is fifteen shillings—more than a laundry maid makes in a month."

"The festival is long over. That might *be* all the vails those men earn this month. Besides, why are you so conversant on the wages of laundry maids?"

"I'm conversant on every aspect of running an aristocratic household. I've been running my father's since before I left the schoolroom, and was raised to understand I'd soon be running Lord Oldfield's households as well. And *you're* trying to change the subject."

"What subject?"

"Your discomfort that I remarked on your kindness."

He folded his arms over his chest. "If you insist upon thinking of me as handsome *and* kind, I shall be forced to bat you away like a fruit fly."

She grinned at him. "Besieged by marriageable young ladies, are you?"

"A dreadful bunch. And no, I've managed to avoid such entanglements thus far. My prickly personality and rough looks have previously been enough to keep them at bay."

"You don't want to keep me at bay," she informed him. "You're my beloved and besotted Mr. Snowfeather."

"I never agreed to act besotted."

"Well, we can't very well present ourselves as a marriage in trouble, can we? Not here in Marrywell. Every matchmaker under the sun would throw herself into reviving the spark in our relationship."

He looked appalled. "We're not to call attention to ourselves whatsoever. Mr. and Mrs. Snowfeather are to be as inconspicuous as possible."

"In that case, we should comport ourselves like a Marrywell success story." She gestured out the window at the fading light. "The sun will set within the hour. The colors are certain to be beautiful. Shall we go and watch the horizon from the follies, my love?"

He grimaced. "I'm going to regret this, aren't I."

"Probably," she agreed cheerfully.

Mr. Frampton sighed. He slid from his chair to hold out his elbow. "Come, then, Mrs. Snowfeather. A sunset awaits us."

CHAPTER 14

As they exited the public house, Mr. Frampton paused next to a fashionable black barouche and gave a coin to the lad watching over it. There was no driver in sight.

"Mind it for another hour, would you?"

Tabitha stared at the empty front seat of the conveyance in surprise. "Never say you drove here *yourself*."

Mr. Frampton shrugged. "It was a nice day."

"It's England. No one ever knows if it's going to *stay* a nice day. Lord Oldfield sent you on a wild goose chase and refused to loan you a driver?"

"I'm certain he'd have lent me all four of his stately coaches if I'd had need of them. That's my barouche. I rarely have the opportunity to take it for a jaunt."

"Your barouche," Tabitha repeated.

She supposed it fit him. Sturdy and practical, with a sporty collapsible roof to take advantage of sun or protect oneself from rain. For the passengers safe in the enclosure, that was. The driver was as exposed to the wind and elements as the pair of horses pulling the carriage.

"Come," said Mr. Frampton. "Wasn't there a sunset you wanted to see?"

Tabitha took his arm. It was strong and warm and steady. A fitting arm for a husband. Her skin flushed with warmth. She fell into step by his side, seamlessly matching his easy rhythm as they ambled up the main street to the botanical gardens.

During the festival, the 400-hectare pleasure gardens swarmed with merrymakers, strolling the grounds or taking picnics by the pond or traversing the hedgerow labyrinth, as she and Mr. Frampton were about to do. The follies were located in the center of the maze.

In the eight years since her come-out, Tabitha had forged her way through this labyrinth so many times, she could make her way through every twist and turn blindfolded.

Not that she wished to miss a single moment of this view. The lush green of the towering hedgerows, the first streaks of pink in the blue sky overhead… and the tall, well-muscled guard dog prowling at her side.

Tabitha tried not to watch him overmuch, but she could not stop herself from stealing glances. His was a handsomeness that came from within. It wasn't his mouth or his cheekbones or his chest, but rather the tightly contained strength and power emanating from every pore.

This was a man who took care of things. And what he'd decided to take care of at the moment… was Tabitha. What could be more attractive than that?

She trusted him with her life, she realized in surprise. This vacant labyrinth in the middle of a plot of land many times the size of Vauxhall Gardens would be the perfect place for a footpad to leap from the shadows, or for a dastardly rakehell to take advantage of an unsuspecting miss.

All perpetrations of violence aside, Mr. Frampton need only spread the idle gossip that Lady Tabitha had jilted her betrothed and taken a holiday by herself under an assumed name, and her reputation would be destroyed overnight… and permanently.

She didn't have to ask him not to do any of those things. He might be ruthless when it came to contracts and negotiations and disputes at gentlemen's clubs, but with her he was only ever protective.

He wasn't just a good man of business. He was a good *man*.

And those could certainly be hard to find.

"Here we are." Light poured into the labyrinth from a break in the hedgerows. Mr. Frampton arched a dark brow. "Lead the way to the folly of your preference."

It was disconcerting to step free of the maze and not be confronted by a swarming crowd of festival-goers. Yet the gardens did not look lonely. Without the hindrance of hundreds or thousands of other people, Tabitha could actually look around and truly register the vast beauty surrounding them.

She pointed toward the tallest folly, designed to look like a miniature castle. It stood two stories high and sported a narrow stone balcony just wide enough for two people to stand side-by-side.

"As you wish." Mr. Frampton led her across the lush green grounds to the large stone folly.

Instead of a wooden doorway, the archway was clear, allowing them to enter without hindrance. Inside, there was no furniture. Just windows everywhere, with views of every angle of the gardens, and curving stone steps leading up to the first floor.

It probably would have made more sense to take the steps in single file, but Tabitha couldn't quite bear to release Mr. Frampton's warm, steady arm just yet. They ascended the flight together, hip-to-hip, their steps in perfect synchronicity.

The first floor was as wide and empty and full of windows as the ground floor beneath it. Any of the vantage points would have a stunning view, but she guided them to the west-facing balcony where the colors of sunset would be at their brightest.

"Do you think me silly for wanting to do this?" she asked as they stepped onto the stone ledge.

He glanced down at her in surprise. "I would think you silly if you did not. One of the best things about my office is the second-floor view of the sunset. I never miss it if I can help it."

She grinned at him. "Me either. A lovely sunset is one of the few things that can tear my attention away from a good book."

"What are the other things?"

"Kittens... chocolate... an invitation to the theatre..."

"Do you have a favorite play?"

"Honestly? My favorite shows are of acrobats and other performers. They don't need a plot to entertain. Their stunts are breathtaking enough on their own."

"I imagine there are those in the audience who cannot tear their gazes from you," he murmured.

She snorted. "Because I am a lady? I should think Prinny and his mistress would make more scandalous fodder."

"I doubt you've been scandalous in your life until today," Mr. Frampton agreed.

"Then why would..." *Oh.* He meant that he found her beautiful, and could not imagine others not being just as entranced.

She gazed up at him, her throat dry.

His intense brown eyes did not leave hers.

They were missing the sunset, and Tabitha did not care one whit. There wasn't quite enough room on the narrow balcony to comfortably face each other, which was one of the only reasons she refrained from throwing herself into Mr. Frampton's arms and begging for a kiss.

The other reason for her restraint was the fear of rejection. She suspected Mr. Frampton wasn't the slightest bit opposed to kissing her senseless... if it weren't for a cursed childhood betrothal remanding her into the possession of his employer.

Mr. Frampton was good at his job. He would not wish to lose it. Which meant abstaining from torrid kisses with the viscount's bride.

No matter how ardently she begged.

Mr. Frampton tore his gaze away and cleared his throat. "Never mind the sunset. Look at the clouds. That one looks like a hedgehog with indigestion."

"It does not," she said with a laugh, then nearly choked on her own chuckle when she caught sight of the cloud he'd been referring to. It absolutely looked like a distempered hedgehog. She pointed in the opposite direction. "And that one looks like a rhinoceros performing ballet."

He glanced in the direction of her finger and grinned with appreciation.

In no time, they were talking over each other, each trying to best the other's discovery with an even more absurd comparison, until they were breathless with laughter, their sides pressed together to prop each other up.

Despite the simplicity, it was one of the best afternoons Tabitha could ever remember having. She'd smiled so much, her cheeks hurt. That hadn't happened in… well… Had it *ever* happened to her before?

Her life was one of privilege, but it was not often one of joy or laughter. These six days with Mr. Frampton weren't merely an escape from the usual weight of impending doom. It was her chance to infuse her spirit with as much happiness as she could, in order to draw upon it throughout the long winter of the rest of her life, subsisting on remembered bits of smiles and sunshine as best she could.

All too soon, the sun dipped below the horizon. The sky was still filled with orange and purple, and clouds that looked like an old man's whiskers, but darkness would fall swiftly.

"Shall we remove to the inn?" she asked as lightly as she could.

The answering weight of his gaze was anything but light. She could feel the absoluteness of his attention, enveloping her, embracing her. Feathering over every inch of her skin, and leaving a delicious wave of gooseflesh in its wake.

"You're certain this is what you want?" His voice was a soft rumble. A warning. A promise.

She nodded. "It's the only thing I want. I shan't change my mind."

He held out his elbow. "Then so it shall be."

She curled her fingers around his arm and held on tight. Next stop: the Blushing Maid Inn.

Where they would spend the night as husband and wife.

CHAPTER 15

As the last of the orange streaks faded from the graying sky, Hudson led Lady Tabitha back to his carriage.

Her grip tightened on his arm and she pointed at the sky. "Look, a shooting star!"

Hudson glanced up just in time to see the white streak disappear. "Make a wish."

"I did." She gave him a bashful smile. "You should, too."

He would not do any such thing. He was far too practical for wishes. Or tried to be. He feared any wish he made in this moment was likely to be of the "I wish I was kissing the woman I'm supposed to be guarding" variety, which was not an act a man hoping to hold onto his well-paying post ought to consider.

And yet, now that the thought had crossed his mind… Oh, who was Hudson bamming? Of course he wanted to kiss her. No other thought had ever crossed his mind whilst gazing down at Lady Tabitha. He had even less control over the direction of his desires when she was holding on to his arm, no more than a perfectly kissable distance away.

"I'll help you into the carriage," he said gruffly.

Her face fell. "Can't I sit up front with you?"

"Up front with me?" he repeated, the words making no sense. "On the driver's perch?"

"Is there not enough room?"

"There's room, but it's…"

Her smile bloomed back, and Hudson's weak protests dissipated like steam from a cup of chocolate.

If she wanted to ride in front, well, why not? She would be exposed to the elements for five minutes at most. It was less than half a mile from the location of this carriage to the inn she'd chosen. And was sitting with him for a moment here in Marrywell any more scandalous than perching atop an open phaeton with an aristocratic suitor in the middle of Hyde Park?

Yes. Yes, it was. An aristocrat could get away with anything. Hudson was a commoner. He wasn't supposed to *talk* with highborn women like Lady Tabitha, much less squeeze onto a rickety bench with her in front of a perfectly serviceable and utterly empty carriage.

But before he could formulate a convincing objection, Hudson found himself seated six feet off the ground, squeezed hip-to-hip in a bench meant for one at the front of his barouche. Lady Tabitha's skirts fluttered against his legs, hiding one of his boots from view.

Not that he was looking at his feet. He was

doing everything he could to keep from staring hungrily at Lady Tabitha… and no doubt failing miserably in the process.

She beamed at him. "May I hold the reins?"

"Do you know how to control my horses?"

"You can teach me."

"Not in two minutes. I'll drive." He set his pair of geldings into motion.

"Are your horses so recalcitrant?" she asked.

"Not particularly," he admitted.

She frowned. "Then why wouldn't you allow me to—"

"Because I don't want to be any more impressed with you than I already am," he snapped.

Her eyes widened. "*You* are impressed by *me*?"

He immediately regretted saying so, and did his best to redirect the conversation to safer ground. "You know how it is between servants and Quality."

"You're still not *my* servant, and you've never toadied to Lord Oldfield."

"How would you know whether I bow and scrape in private?"

She snorted. "Because I've seen how you look at him in public. You tolerate him, at best. I would guess you believe you'd make a better viscount than the viscount, but the most likely scenario is that there's no guessing necessary. I'm sure it's fact. I'd wager you already perform all of Lord Oldfield's tasks for him, and likely better than the viscount would if left to his own devices."

"I cannot sit in the House of Lords."

"Does Oldfield?"

"No," Hudson admitted.

Yet another way his employer was feckless and irresponsible. Oldfield was better acquainted with the contours of a dozen debutantes' bosoms than he was familiar with the laws and debates of the time.

Did Hudson think he'd make a better viscount? Yes. Was this opinion because he already performed the associated tasks, or was the reason because he wished he was the one betrothed to his employer's bride?

Also yes.

Hudson certainly wouldn't have sent some other man to fetch her. He would've done everything in his power to ensure Lady Tabitha entered a union with him willingly to begin with. A runaway bride did not mean a failure on behalf of the bride. A runaway bride signified a mésalliance. If Oldfield were the right husband for her, she would not have fled out of desperation to avoid him.

She certainly wasn't running from Hudson. She was plastered next to him as if they were conjoined at the hip and shoulder.

He had never seen her willingly step within arm's reach of the viscount.

"We're here," Hudson announced as he pulled the carriage to a stop in front of the Blushing Maid Inn.

He leapt to the ground. After handing the reins to one of the inn's waiting stable lads, Hudson turned back around to help Lady Tabitha down from the driver's perch—just in time to see her leap airborne, as he had done.

Reacting purely out of instinct, he dashed forward to catch her, rather than allow her to find her own landing. Her body slid against his as she slowly eased to the ground.

Once Lady Tabitha was safely on solid earth, Hudson immediately released his hold of her. Or tried to, very hard. Or meant to try to. Felt obligated to release her. And felt simultaneously the utter incapacity to do anything more than keep his arms right where they were, wrapped tight about her waist.

Her arms were conveniently still about his neck, her smiling face upturned at a distance absolutely ripe for kissing.

Not that he was going to kiss her. Probably. That was to say, definitely not. Was he? His insides were a flutter and his mind had emptied of all coherent thought. He was certain he had very strong reasons to let her go before his mouth tasted hers, but at the moment all such logical considerations escaped him.

A throat cleared just behind him. "Are Mister and Missus in need of a room for the night?"

Right. Mister and Missus. A thing Hudson and Lady Tabitha certainly were not. They were only pretending.

He peeled himself away from her and turned to the innkeeper. "Actually—"

"We already have a room," Lady Tabitha interrupted, aiming her dazzling smile at the innkeeper. "This is my darling husband, Mr. Snowfeather. I can show him to our quarters."

Hudson braced himself for the innkeeper's inevitable skepticism, but to his surprise, the man smiled cheerfully and welcomed them inside as though all married couples in Marrywell regularly leapt off of driver's perches into each other's arms.

"Er," Hudson managed. "My barouche…"

"We'll carry up any luggage, and take good care of your horses and your conveyance," the innkeeper assured him. "Just ring when you want the vehicle brought round, and we'll manage the rest."

Lady Tabitha wrapped her arm around Hudson's, and batted her eyelashes up at him. "Come, my love."

Hudson didn't know which he liked best: the thought of coming, or the idea of being Lady Tabitha's true love.

Neither was a likely occurrence. He glared down at her quellingly.

She twinkled up at him all the brighter.

"Our rooms?" he growled.

"This way, darling." She tugged him up a full flight of stairs before collapsing against him in giggles. "The innkeeper was *so* relieved to hear you were my husband. The poor soul would suffer an apoplexy if he knew—"

"Shh." Hudson placed a finger against her lips. "Not here."

She winked, kissed the finger pressing against her lips, then spun down the closest corridor to unlock the second door on the left. "Here we are then, Mr. Snowfeather."

Hudson crossed the threshold right behind her.

At first glance, the rooms were very clean, very pretty, and very… compact. They were standing in a parlor not much larger than his barouche. It barely fit a narrow sofa for two, and a small tea table with two slender armchairs. He hoped the delicately carved walnut wouldn't splinter around him.

"Perfect, isn't it?" pronounced Lady Tabitha rapturously.

Perfectly dangerous. Now that Hudson wouldn't be pining from afar, it would be harder than ever to hide the depth of his feelings for her. Sharing space with Lady Tabitha felt too easy. He thoroughly enjoyed every second of her company. And *she* seemed to enjoy... well, everything. Lady Tabitha was the opposite of spoilt. She was adaptable and resilient and allowed nothing to keep her spirits down for long.

A knock sounded at the door. Hudson opened it at once.

Lady Tabitha's eyes widened in surprise at the sight of a quartet of footmen hauling multiple heavy valises into the tiny parlor.

"What's this?" she asked in obvious confusion.

"Our trunks," he replied dryly, tipping each of the footmen a vail before closing the door behind them.

"But..." she stammered, her wide eyes still taking in the tower of leather valises. "How long did you think it would take to find me?"

"Hours, at most."

"And didn't you say you'd intended to pop me into the carriage and head right back home?"

"That's correct."

"Then what on earth is all of this? You cannot possibly require this many changes of clothes per hour. Even a dandy like Beau Brummell wouldn't need—"

Hudson opened the topmost valise.

Three neatly packed columns of fashionable ladies' day dresses greeted them.

"You brought me clothes?" Lady Tabitha stepped forward and pressed one of the gowns to her bosom. "My *favorite* clothes?"

"Mary Frances helped," he said gruffly. "I simply told her what I wanted, and she put the trunks together."

Lady Tabitha stared at the pile of luggage. "What did you tell her you wanted?"

"Suitable garments for all weather possibilities, and enough variety to last for weeks, if necessary."

"Just in case?"

"I try to always be prepared."

She wrapped her free arm around his shoulders and kissed his cheek. "Thank you. I fear I am currently wearing the entirety of my travel wardrobe, so your forethought is serendipitous indeed."

Hudson's cheek burned where she'd kissed it. All of him burned for her. He was glad to have pleased her. The happiness radiating from her face made him feel like a knight who had vanquished a dragon.

Dangerous thoughts filled him.

Thoughts like: if Lady Tabitha got to know the real Hudson over the course of this week, might she perhaps decide he suited her far better than her unwanted betrothed?

Thoughts like: if they *were* to fall in love, in truth,

not for pretend, then perhaps somehow the always-prepared man of business could find a way for such a union to work, without ruining either of their lives.

"We should get some sleep," he informed her, keeping his voice firm and impersonal to hide the direction of his traitorous thoughts.

She dropped her favorite gown back onto the pile as if the material had caught fire in her hands. "Straight away."

"*Separately*," he added, in case there was any doubt.

She sent him a sunny smile and pushed open the door to the sleeping quarters. "About that…"

One bed. There was *just one bed.*

Barely big enough to hold Hudson, much less Hudson and Lady Tabitha. He stared at it in horror. In want. In agony.

"I'll sleep on the sofa," he said quickly.

"You won't fit on the sofa," she pointed out.

"I'll sleep on the floor."

"*No one* can sleep well on a hardwood floor. You'll sleep with me."

"I won't sleep."

"Then rest." She began to unpin her hair. "Relax, Mr. Snowfeather. I'm already compromised, if you wish to be technical about such things. Sleeping atop the same mattress cannot worsen an already ruined reputation."

Sleeping was the least of Hudson's concerns. He willed himself to appear utterly disinterested in debauching the feathers out of her, right here and now.

He'd known this terrible plan would require them to pretend. He would simply have to pretend every atom of his being wasn't straining toward her in abject longing, burning to act as husband and wife as more than a jest. God help him. Hudson swallowed hard.

It was going to be a very, very long night.

CHAPTER 16

*T*abitha awoke with her face smashed up against Mr. Frampton's strong back.

She jerked away out of reflex, horrified to think that instead of running her fingers over those rippling muscles, she'd drooled all over his nightshirt instead.

The sharp movement of Tabitha jerking backward caused the blanket to move with her—which in turn tilted Mr. Frampton from his side to his back. And revealed an unmistakable ridge in the tented blanket.

Before Tabitha could so much as blink, Mr. Frampton's eyes flew open wide and the pillow beneath his head swooped to cover his groin.

"I told you this was a terrible idea," he growled.

She beamed at him. "Good morning, husband."

He closed his eyes and groaned.

Tabitha's smile grew wider. This didn't feel terrible at all. The opposite. This was glorious. She'd never before woken up next to a man, and honestly never expected to have such an occasion. To the best of her knowledge, aristocratic lords and ladies always slept alone in their separate chambers, coming together only briefly for the act of begetting the next heir.

With Mr. Frampton, her first experience in the same bed as a man hadn't been loathsome or terrifying in the least. Yes, he'd ordered her to stay on her side of the bed—which she'd clearly failed to do. He either hadn't noticed her transgression, or chose to allow her to sleep snuggled up next to him like a kitten rather than wake her for a scolding.

He opened one eye. "Why are you still in bed? Go and get ready."

"You're still in bed," she pointed out.

"I need a minute. *Go.*"

She pushed the blanket from her nightrail. His pupils dilated and he closed his eyes tight. She swung her feet off of the mattress and onto the wooden floor.

"I… shall need some help when it's time to lace up my gown."

"I may be ready by then," he mumbled. "Or dead. I may never open my eyes again."

Tabitha blew him a kiss—why not? He couldn't see her—and padded over to the washbasin atop the nightstand to ready herself for the day. She exchanged her nightrail for a fresh shift, and shimmied into a rose-colored day dress. In the looking-glass, Mr. Frampton made several agonized expressions but never once opened his eyes.

There was no hope of fastening her gown by herself, so Tabitha quickly gave up trying. She arranged her hair as best she could, then turned back to the bed. "I'm ready for you now."

Mr. Frampton let out a tortured moan. "Never utter that phrase to me again."

"But I—"

"Turn around."

She turned around. Mr. Frampton was still visible in the looking-glass. He visibly sucked in a deep breath, then flung the pillow at the headboard and swung his legs out of bed.

Her mouth fell open. "You slept in your trousers?"

"I should've loaned *you* some," he muttered, and stalked over to where she stood, the bottoms of his trousers poking out from beneath his calf-length white cotton nightshirt. "Don't move. I'll do this as quickly as I can."

She didn't move.

His fingers were neither as light nor as swift as her lady's maid. Yet his heavier touch did not feel clumsy, but rather… slow and sensual. Gooseflesh rippled across her skin at each brush of his fingers. Inch by inch, the gaping gown tightened across her bodice. He tied the knot, then leapt away as though the silk ribbons had tried to bind him to her.

"Wait for me in the parlor," he ordered.

She spun to face him, her skirts swirling against his nightshirt and trousers. "Are we going on adventure?"

"Hasn't this been adventure enough?"

"With you, I doubt the adventure ever ends," she said softly.

His jaw worked, then he pointed toward the open bedchamber door. "Parlor. *Now*. I'll be there in just a moment."

Tabitha nodded dutifully and headed toward the parlor. No sooner had she crossed the threshold when the bedroom door closed tight behind her.

True to his word, Mr. Frampton did not tarry long with his morning ablutions. In scant minutes, he emerged from the bedchamber dapper and freshly shaved, with casual buckskins stretched across his powerful legs. Beneath his dark grey coat was a burgundy waistcoat. The silk threads of its embroidered edges perfectly matched the deep rose of Tabitha's gown.

She could not help but wonder if such serendipitous coordination was happenstance, or if Mr. Frampton had planned out every stitch of the clothing in their trunks with the same precision he executed all the other tasks he regularly undertook.

"Come on, then." He held out his elbow. "We'll request to have our breakfast bundled for travel."

She hurried to take his arm. "Where are we going?"

"On an adventure."

In no time, they were out of the inn and back onto the main street. Mr. Frampton strolled with Tabitha on one arm and the brown-paper-wrapped parcel containing their breakfast beneath the other.

She did not ask again where they were going. Her life had been devoid of spontaneity—even her future husband had been chosen for her before she was even born—and she found she quite enjoyed the element of surprise.

Tabitha glanced at each building they passed

with curiosity. Would this be the one they stopped at? No. None of the taverns, pubs, inns, and public houses. Not the brewers' field or the botanical gardens.

Soon enough, they were headed out of town altogether. There were no more people or buildings. Just a thick green woods… and a narrow dirt walking path she'd never noticed until just now.

"How did you know this was here?" she asked in wonder.

Mr. Frampton sent her an arrogant look, as if to say there was nothing in this world that escaped his notice.

Tabitha was inclined to believe it.

The path was likely intended for single pedestrians, but they strode along the rocky soil hip-to-hip. Leaves rustled overhead with the breeze. Other than occasional birdsong, little broke the peace and quiet.

That, or Tabitha's heart was thundering so loud, a parade of elephants could have been stampeding behind her, and she would not have heard them.

Mr. Frampton's steps slowed seconds before she registered the soft sound of running water. The next curve in the path took them beside a burbling river, its surface shimmering beneath the dappled sunlight.

He disengaged their joined arms in order to brush off the top of a knee-high fallen log, more than wide enough to support two derrières.

She gasped in delight. "A riverside picnic?"

"Sit," he replied gruffly.

She sat, and grinned at him as he unwrapped

their breakfast, balancing the brown paper and its contents on his lap. This was nothing like the five-course meals she was accustomed to, or the countless candlelit dinner parties she attended every year.

This was the most romantic meal of her entire life.

She selected a bun followed by slices of fresh fruit. They rested shoulder-to-shoulder in quiet companionship, listening to the breeze and the birds, and gazing at the reflection of white clouds and blue sky in the sparkling water as they broke their fast.

Mostly gazed at nature. Tabitha stole several sidelong glances at Mr. Frampton between bites, and several times caught him doing the same.

As their bellies filled, the silence vanished, and they fell into easy conversation. The warmth of the day, the sweet smells of spring, the crispness of the breeze... anything but the real reason they were here. That Tabitha had run away, rather than wed her intended. That Mr. Frampton would lose his post if he didn't deliver her back into Viscount Oldfield's clutches, safe and sound.

"Why aren't you married?" she blurted out.

He raised his brows. "How do you know I am not?"

"You're not wearing a ring," she stammered, her cheeks heating at having been caught looking.

"Perhaps I was once married, but no longer have a wife."

"Did you lose someone you loved?" she asked in horror.

"No." He turned his gaze back to the river. "I have never had anyone to lose."

"You were an only child, like me?"

"I was an orphan, unlike you."

"I'm so sorry," she whispered.

He shrugged. "My parents were gone from my life long before I had a chance to know or miss them."

Somehow, she suspected this was not fully true. He might never have known them, but that did not mean they hadn't left mother-and-father-sized holes in his heart all the same.

"You were raised in an orphanage?"

"For a few years. Chimneysweep by the age of five, and a damn good one until I grew too big to fit into tiny spaces. They tried to feed me less to keep me small, but when a body decides to grow… They found other tasks for me."

"'They' meaning the orphanage?"

"I'd left that place far behind. 'They' meaning, whichever band of morally questionable vagabonds happened to take me in."

Her jaw dropped. "You became a criminal?"

"I became adept at any number of ethically dubious exploits designed to fill my belly and my pockets."

"But you could have been sent to gaol!"

"And I was, several times, before the age of twelve," he agreed, as if admitting to a fault no more noteworthy than not having tied his cravat correctly. "I turned out to be very good at many things. A cutpurse, a ruffian, an enforcer in the criminal underworld…"

Tabitha narrowed her eyes. Every word carried

the ring of truth, yet she could not help but suspect Mr. Frampton was doing his best to convince her that he was not the sort of man she ought to be alone with—or even in whose company a lady of her status ought to spend any time at all.

Yet she'd never felt safer or more at peace than she did right now, beside this babbling brook, perched on a fallen log next to an admitted childhood felon, who had grown into a man so burly and powerful he struck fear into the hearts of everyone unlucky enough to catch his eye...

Except on the occasions when he happened to exchange his usual battles for the bank of a river, upon which he shared plums and biscuits with a runaway whose rose-colored dress he had taken great pains to match with the embroidery of his waistcoat.

"How did you go from footpad to reputable man of business?" she asked.

He looked at her in amusement. "What makes you think I'm a reputable anything? My utility for my employer lies in the fact that I see and do things that others will not. I have made fortunes for us both many times over. He cannot lose me. Not until he learns to stop spending the riches I bring him."

"You're *rich*?" she said in surprise.

"As Croesus," he agreed.

She tried to reframe what she thought she knew of him. "Then why work for anyone?"

"It amuses me. I like the challenge. And I fully admit, the only reason the best opportunities cross my desk is because I'm Viscount Oldfield's man of business."

That made sense. Being the right hand to a lord would put Mr. Frampton in the thick of things in a way he'd never have access to without that connection.

"Besides," he continued, "If you're imagining I could become the sort of idle gentleman you're accustomed to seeing in the ton, get that notion out of your head right now. Entrée in the beau monde is determined by blood, not by the size of one's pocketbook."

She scoffed. "There are countless nouveau-riche heiresses whose dowries come from—"

"Fathers who shimmied up chimneys and picked pockets? I doubt it. If their coffers contain enough gold, the door to the haut ton might open slightly to allow in those who stand just one rung below them on the ladder of aristocracy. But you will never find a scullery maid or a stable boy holding court with lords and ladies."

That was true, but... not the whole truth. It was as if Mr. Frampton were trying to scare her off.

Or trying to put himself in his place.

"*You* rub shoulders with the aristocracy," she reminded him. "You've been present at several of the same gatherings as I have—"

"As a member of staff, not as an honored guest," he pointed out dryly.

"That's not always the case," she insisted. "A few weeks ago, when we were here in Marrywell together before Lord Oldfield arrived, you and I attended every one of the festivities together. Not a single soul raised their eyebrows at your presence."

"Marrywell's annual matchmaking festival is an unusual situation," he admitted. "But it is not representative of real life. Perhaps you're right. I could have courted any number of milkmaids and green country misses. But how many dukes and earls do you think would have accepted my request to marry their precious daughters?"

He did not say *or marquesses*, but she felt the unspoken words hang between them. Mr. Frampton was saying that Marrywell didn't matter, then or now. It would never be seemly for a man like him to express interest in someone as highborn as Tabitha.

Yet the thought of him courting all those milkmaids and country misses threatened to turn her stomach into acid.

He folded up the now-empty square of brown paper and brushed a few stray crumbs from his leather-clad thighs. "Breakfast is over. We should go."

"Wait," she said desperately. "I'm not ready yet."

He sighed and inclined his head. "I suppose we could take the trail a little farther."

"No. I have a better idea." She bent over to untie her half-boots. She'd dreamed of spontaneity. Why not start now?

"What in the devil are you doing?" he asked in alarm.

She grinned up at him and tossed her boots aside. "Come and catch me."

And with that, she ran into the water.

CHAPTER 17

*H*udson stared after her in disbelief as the woman he most desired ran laughingly past him to splash into the river.

If Lady Tabitha had haunted his dreams before, the memory of her fine clothes plastered to her curves would never leave his every waking thought.

He should have foreseen this. He should have *stopped* this. He should not be… tossing aside his own boots and stockings and coat in order to chase after her into the water, as though they were a pair of lovers on holiday at the sea shore.

The moment his bare foot broke the surface, the freezing cold water shocked every nerve in his body—but it was too late to change course. Momentum and gravity and (yes, let's face it) the unquenchable desire to be with Lady Tabitha vaulted him forward, despite the frigid temperatures.

Perhaps his body acclimated quickly, or perhaps his extremities had simply gone numb, because the moment he reached her side, Hudson forgot all about the cold. If anything, heat infused his limbs at his proximity to her wet body and the forbiddenness of their actions.

"Not much of a river," he growled. "The deepest part barely comes up to my stomach."

Lady Tabitha fluttered her eyelashes at him. "Oh, dear. Were you hoping to have to save me?"

"That's not what I—"

She took a comically large breath and launched herself backwards into the water, quickly sinking below the surface.

He knew she was teasing—knew she was *baiting* him—but he was hooked all the same. Before he had time to form conscious thought, Hudson dove into the spot where she'd disappeared, pulling her into his arms and dragging her to the surface until their heads bobbed free of the water.

But he didn't let go.

Neither did she.

Their legs tangled together beneath the water. Not that Hudson could see their feet. Lady Tabitha's skirts floated up to her hips, blocking the view… and filling his brain with images of what he might see if *he* were to sink below the surface.

Dangerous thoughts. Intoxicating thoughts. He had no idea what he was doing. His shoulders might be above water, but Hudson was in far over his head.

Lady Tabitha's arms held him loosely, her fingers idly clutching the cotton of his shirt that had billowed out beneath the back of his waistcoat when he'd dived into the water.

Hudson's hands were about her waist. Whether to hold her steady, or to prevent her swirling skirts from floating up any higher, he couldn't say. Either way, his only mission was to keep her safe. From the elements. From him.

Lady Tabitha was close enough to kiss. Hudson had never wanted anything more in his life. She was smiling at him, staring up at him, the silk of her bodice molded to her bosom as droplets of water danced tantalizingly over her décolletage. Oh Lord, he should definitely not be staring at her breasts.

Her plump, wet breasts with their erect nipples pointing straight at his pounding heart.

Especially not whilst his face was mere inches from hers, and there was no hiding the direction of his gaze. He forced himself to meet her eyes and only made it as far as her lips. Also plump. And rosy. And parted, as if awaiting a kiss. *His* kiss.

"Well?" she asked softly. "Are you going to do it or not?"

Not. Definitely not.

Such betrayal would mean his post. She was betrothed to Hudson's employer, for God's sake. And to those of her circles, Hudson was nothing more than a servant. Their classes did not mix.

Even if Hudson had been born a viscount like Lord Oldfield, Hudson still couldn't kiss another man's bride. It was worse than ungentlemanly. It was a date to duel at dawn, and to risk his own life. If Viscount Oldfield didn't kill him, Lady Tabitha's father the marquess would be next in line to take aim with a pistol.

Those were the reasons why not. They were very good reasons. Wise reasons.

And right now, Hudson didn't give a flying fig about any of them.

He answered her impertinent question not with words, but by crashing his mouth against hers. Devouring her. Offering up himself in equal measure. Giving, taking, exploding into a thousand pieces.

The kiss was everything he'd hoped and feared it would be. Bliss. Torture. He hauled her closer so that her wet bosom pillowed against his hard chest. It wasn't merely the light brush of two pairs of lips anymore. It was a full body kiss. It was the river itself, swirling the kiss around them, dragging them deeper into the current.

He lost track of time. Lost all conscious thought. He was no longer a man, but a tempest of want and need and desire. He took a kiss for every time he'd awoken with a start, sweating and trembling and hard as stone. He took a kiss for every teasing smile, every tinkle of laughter. For every drop of water in the river and every invisible star in the skies high above.

He tore his mouth free from hers with a gasp. The loss felt like drowning. As though her lips were the oxygen that gave him life, and without her kiss he was doomed to die.

Panting, he rested his forehead against hers and prayed for fortitude.

"That... felt real to me," she murmured.

Hudson did not answer. He didn't have to. Nothing had ever felt more real than their kiss. To deny it would be to deny his own soul. And she knew it.

"I was thinking," she began.

He closed his eyes. He had categorically *not* been thinking, which was why the bare legs of his employer's bride were wrapped loosely about his hips, her derrière perched lightly atop his thighs as their shoulders bobbed just above the water.

"Don't say it," he begged, his voice gravelly with desire. "Whatever it is. We should not."

She pressed forward, holding him a little tighter. The tip of her nose brushed his. Her smile, kissing distance from his own parted lips.

"We're pretending to be husband and wife," she whispered. "What if we didn't pretend?"

"What?" he asked hoarsely.

"Just until you take me home," she said quickly. "While we're here. While we're someone else. Why not live like it?"

"Lady Tabitha—"

"Just Tabitha. No more 'lady', please. Today and for the rest of the week, I am Mrs. Tabitha Snowfeather. Your temporary wife. In name, *and* in body, if you'd like to—"

Hudson did the only thing he could to stop the flow of words.

He kissed her.

This was the worst possible consequence of his rash actions. Instead of slapping his face and pushing him away, she was tempting him with a cornucopia of forbidden fruit.

His, in name and body, if he'd like that? There was nothing he wanted more. The knowledge that he was not the only one fighting the pull of desire only fanned the flames higher. He'd known for years that he wanted her. And he hadn't the slightest clue that she wanted him, too.

Until now.

What was he meant to do with this knowledge? Kiss her, as he was doing now? Debauch her, as she requested? Live like husband and wife for one perfect, idyllic week? And then hand her off to some other man, doomed to live out the rest of his days beneath the same roof as the woman he loved and her new husband, knowing it would never again be Hudson's lips that she kissed, or Hudson's bed that she shared?

He broke the kiss. Broke free from her embrace. Did his best to break the spell enchanting them.

"No," he said firmly. "You don't know what you're asking."

"I do," she insisted.

"You do not. You're a virgin—"

"I won't be for long, one way or the other. Why not enjoy it, with you?"

He grimaced. "No good can come of—"

"Can you look me in the eyes and tell me those kisses weren't *good*?"

Of course they weren't good. They were transcendental. A blessing, a curse, a thousand wishes coming true all at once. There would never be another kiss half as perfect. He was ruined forever.

And if Hudson had any hope of surviving the rest of his life employed beneath the same roof, he had to stop the madness right here and now. He couldn't undo the kisses. Would die rather than change a single moment. But he couldn't give in to anything more. He was destined to be her protector, her guardian angel, her bodyguard, her watchdog… but not her husband.

"Come," he said roughly, pulling her to her feet. "That's enough make-believe for one day."

"If you change your mind," she said quietly. "You know where to find me."

Of course he did: all week long, she'd be inches away from him. Every night, sharing the same bed. His deepest fantasy, ready and willing to come to life. In the palm of his hand.

How the devil was he supposed to resist that?

CHAPTER 18

Hudson expected Lady Tabitha to argue about the abrupt end to their picnic, but to his surprise, she exited the river at once, and with good cheer. It was Hudson who suddenly wished to remain in the water.

The sight of her bending over to slip on her shoes, the sodden fabric of her gown clinging to every luscious curve… His throat went dry, and he gained a new appreciation for waist-high freezing water.

But he couldn't tarry in the river forever. Hudson took a deep, bracing breath and hauled himself ashore, realizing with dread that his wet clothes would outline everything he wished to keep secret.

Then again, who was he bamming? Lady Tabitha knew he desired her. Five minutes ago, she'd been straddling his lap whilst Hudson gloried in her kisses. Any further proof would be redundant at this point.

Self-consciousness caused him to turn away all the same as he pulled on his boots.

"Ready to return to the inn?" he asked without glancing over his shoulder.

"I'll race you," she replied, and took off running.

Hudson let out a yelp of surprise, hopping forward on his one booted foot while trying to shove on the other boot in order to give chase.

By the time he caught up with her, she had almost reached the edge of the woods. He grabbed her from behind, causing her to squeal with laughter. Momentum carried them both forward, and Hudson narrowly avoided tumbling her to the ground. Upon the soft green grass, any number of exceptionally bad ideas could easily take place.

Luckily for them both, Lady Tabitha put on a burst of speed, and Hudson was forced to chase after her. They broke free from the woods together, arm-in-arm, looking like a pair of drowned rats and laughing like children.

When they arrived back at the inn, to say the proprietor was befuddled by their sodden appearance would be an understatement. The poor soul's confusion only grew when Lady Tabitha blithely informed him that she and Mr. Snowfeather had been caught in the rain. The sun hadn't stopped shining since the moment Hudson awoke in a bed next to Lady Tabitha.

He ordered a pair of hot baths and dragged her up the stairs to their rooms before the proprietor's gaze could wander over any more of Hudson's pretend wife's wet form.

When the baths arrived, the two tubs barely fit side by side in the small parlor. Lady Tabitha raised her slender brows at him with interest. He scowled at her reprovingly and managed to drag a privacy screen between the two tubs.

"Spoilsport," she murmured. Her eyes twinkled merrily.

"Bathe," he ordered. "You need to get warm and dry."

She held out her arms and did her best to look helpless. "I fear I've left my lady's maid at home."

God help him, Hudson was not strong enough for this. But she was right. If she'd needed help to don the gown when it was still clean and dry, peeling the wet fabric off her body definitely required another pair of hands.

Hudson's hands.

He clenched his jaw and prayed for fortitude as he set about his task. Every new inch of exposed skin seemed to add an additional inch to Hudson's ever-growing erection that soon would not be contained by any trousers, no matter how tight.

He stayed firmly behind Lady Tabitha, willing her not to see how deeply she affected him—and willing himself to keep his hungry eyes far away from the front of her nude body. Just glimpsing her bare shoulders and delicate spine and lush derrière was more than enough to drive him mad with want.

He could barely keep his wits together long enough to fling himself on the other side of the privacy screen to undress for his own bath. Especially knowing Lady Tabitha was completely nude —and unabashedly willing—on the other side of that screen.

Hudson sank into the hot sudsy water, torn between slipping his hand around his cock to relieve the pressure… and the risk that Lady Tabitha might overhear some involuntary sound and realize exactly what he was doing.

Waiting until nightfall wouldn't help, either. He could hardly masturbate with her in the same bed. He would simply have to grind his teeth and hold it together until the end of the week when some other man took her off his hands.

And then he could punch a hole in the closest wall and bang his head against his desk for putting himself in this situation to begin with.

"How's your bath?" came a light, cheerful voice from the other side of the screen. "Do you even fit in the tub?"

Not all of him. Hudson sank down as low as he could. "Lady Tabitha—"

"*Tabitha.* I told you. Please drop the 'lady' nonsense."

"You're not Mrs. Snowfeather."

"But I am Tabitha, and I've given you leave to address me as such. I never pegged you to be such a stick-in-the-mud for aristocratic manners, Mr. Frampton."

He let out a sigh of defeat between clenched teeth and gave up. "Hudson."

"Hudson," she repeated in wonder.

He could hear her smile in her voice. She sounded as though she were tasting his name, savoring it like the finest of sweets.

Oh, how he wished they really were just Tabitha and Hudson, two random people absolutely unencumbered by anyone else's wishes, free to seek love and happiness in each other's arms if they so wished!

Instead, he was an extremely aroused, very grumpy man who should never have agreed to this cockamamie scheme. Even if it was turning out to be one of the best weeks of Hudson's life. This was not his bride, or his holiday to have. He knew better. The real world would intrude on them both before they knew it.

He finished his bath in record time, drying and dressing himself as fast as he could before Tabitha needed his help donning a fresh day dress.

As before, she managed into her stays and shift by herself, but could not tie the back of her gown. Hudson performed the task as quickly as possible… which turned out to be very slowly indeed. It was hard to rush the process when he wanted to be as close to her as possible. She was so warm and soft, and smelled so fresh and clean. He would be happy to stand here and breathe in her essence, just like this, until their week together was through.

Tonight, when they climbed in bed together, he would remain firmly on his side of the mattress. But he wouldn't sleep a wink. He couldn't bear to. If these scant days were to be the only moments he shared with Tabitha before she belonged to someone else, Hudson wanted to savor every moment of it.

He would listen to her breathe and watch her sleep and wish like hell that these six days could last the rest of their lives.

CHAPTER 19

*T*abitha awoke nestled into Hudson for the second morning in a row, but this time was different: instead of her face smashed against his wide back, her cheek lay atop his arm and her forehead rested against his chest. She had never felt so warm and cozy and… safe.

A woman could get used to mornings like this.

She held as still as possible, determined not to break the spell. His heart was steady as he slept, its rhythm strong and comforting. His large, muscular body emanated heat and strength, as if she were a kitten cuddling a sleeping lion.

He smelled phenomenal. It wasn't a cologne, nor quite matched the soap from their baths. It was a scent all his own, subtle and masculine. Tabitha wanted to wrap it around her like a blanket. Carry it with her for comfort, long after he was gone, to remind her what it felt like to be safe, and happy, and at peace.

She tilted her chin forward until her mouth brushed his chest, in order to press her lips against his heartbeat in a secret kiss.

"You're awake," he murmured into her hair.

She felt the rumble of his voice against her lips and jerked her mouth away from his chest.

"*You're* awake?" she managed, mortified at being caught kissing him when she thought he was asleep.

"I have been so for an hour," he admitted.

Tabitha frowned. "Then why are you still in bed?"

He pressed a kiss against the top of her head. "I didn't want to wake you."

Of course he couldn't rise from bed without waking her. She'd been using his arm as a pillow.

Impulsively, she flung her own arms around him and squeezed him in the tightest hug she could. How was this man the most thoughtful, caring person ever to enter her life? When had "Oldfield's guard dog" become *her* guardian angel?

Rather than push her away, Hudson chuckled softly and wrapped her in his arms and held her close. "Good morning, Mrs. Snowfeather."

"Good morning, Mr. Snowfeather," Tabitha replied automatically, but a worm of doubt dulled the edges of her happiness.

Was he just pretending? Going along with the ruse, as she'd asked him to do? Or, like her, was their unexpected connection the realest, truest thing to ever come into his life?

She tilted her head up to face him.

His gaze was soft and warm, his lips inches from hers. "Is there something you want?"

"I want you to kiss me," she whispered. "And mean it."

Hunger filled his eyes. His mouth slanted over hers without hesitation.

This kiss was as dizzying and powerful as the ones they'd shared in the river, yet different. Deeper. Truer. As though he was still holding back, but much less so than before. As if every kiss shattered another brick in the wall of societal expectations separating them, bringing them one step closer to destroying the barrier forever.

Tabitha wanted whatever was on the other side. Wanted *him*. Wanted this. Couldn't bear for the moment to end, for the week to conclude, for the tides of real life to envelop her in its vicious current and drag her into its dark depths to die miserable and cold.

She knew her duty. Would do her duty. But first, she would experience what it might be like not to have been born a marquess's daughter. To have the freedom to decide for herself, to steer her own ship, to choose whom to give her body to.

As for giving away her heart, she suspected she had little choice in that matter, whether as a lady or a runaway pretending to be a commoner. Tabitha had no power to decide where her heart should lie.

It already belonged to the man whose mouth and tongue melded with hers.

His presence didn't just banish the helplessness and desperation that had clung to her since birth. His kisses made her feel like a goddess. Powerful. Capable. Desirable.

Maybe even worthy of love.

A knock sounded at the exterior door leading to the corridor, startling them from their kiss.

Tabitha blinked, disoriented. "Who would call at… what time is it?"

"Early." Hudson released her from his arms with gentle care and rolled from the bed. "It must be important."

"How can it be? No one knows we're here. Perhaps someone is lost."

"More likely, it is the news I was expecting. I asked one of my men to update me about your father, and keep me abreast of any change in his condition."

Terror flooded Tabitha's veins, cold and slimy. She scrambled from the bed, her previously relaxed limbs now graceless and jerking. "Something happened to my father?"

"I didn't say that." But he was already striding toward the door, where a folded missive poked underneath.

She hurried after him, fear and self-recrimination tensing every muscle and enshrouding every inch of skin in gooseflesh. Whilst she was gallivanting about carefree, feeling truly happy for the first time in her life—her father was at home in his sickbed.

Dying.

Or worse… already dead.

"Lord save me," she whispered. "I am the worst daughter. I should never have run away from the altar. I should have fulfilled Papa's dying wish while he was still alive to see it. I should never have put my personal revulsion above his altruistic desire to—"

Hudson's eyes snapped up from the letter to arrest hers. "He's fine."

She swayed. "W-what?"

Hudson grabbed her arms to steady her. "He's the same as he was when you left. No better, no worse. Dr. Collins stands by his estimation of yet another month or so before you lose your father. Don't fret. The marquess is still alive."

Tabitha collapsed against Hudson's chest and sobbed.

He folded his arms around her protectively and let her cry in silence.

"He must be so worried about me," she mumbled, salty tears wetting her lips.

"He's annoyed," Hudson said flatly. "He believes you're rebelling against his good judgment, and has already advised the viscount to keep a tight leash once you're wed."

Tabitha let out a choking laugh. Foolish girl. Of course her father wasn't worrying about her. When had he ever? It was just another misstep in the eternal dance of Tabitha disappointing her father by having thoughts of her own, and scrambling to win back his favor however she could.

She lifted her face from Hudson's chest and wiped her tears away. "Still. A good daughter would never have—"

"You don't want to know how I think a good *father* should act toward his daughter."

She blinked up at him. "You no longer believe my week of freedom to be folly?"

"I hate everything about your situation," Hudson replied, then lifted her chin with his knuckle. "Except for the stolen moments I share with you."

She sucked in a shuddering breath and wrapped her arms about his neck. "In that case…"

Their mouths came together with hunger. But Tabitha was no longer content with mere kisses. Two days of their short week were already gone. This was her one chance to know love… and pleasure. Her only opportunity to be with Hudson. To be free, and safe, and happy.

She was not going to waste a single moment of it.

CHAPTER 20

*A*n hour later, Tabitha gazed at Hudson over the breakfast table in the inn's public dining room.

His eyes narrowed. "What?"

"Just thinking about how we might spend the day," she answered innocently.

If anything, the suspicious look on his face grew more pronounced. He leaned back from his empty plate and crossed his arms over his wide chest. "What did you have in mind?"

She fluttered her eyelashes at him. "Perhaps an encore at the river? With a picnic blanket this time?"

"Tabitha—"

"Or we can go back upstairs. The bed was nice and comfortable. I wouldn't mind spending another hour or two beneath the covers… with you."

"Tabitha, a few kisses are one thing—"

"Mrs. *Snowfeather*," she reminded him firmly. "And unless I'm mistaken, one of the most common activities enjoyed by a Mr. and Mrs. is the act of—"

"Sightseeing," he interrupted. Hudson pulled her to her feet and tucked her arm securely around his. "A man and a woman on holiday would not waste the long trip by tarrying indoors."

"Remind me never to go on honeymoon with *you*," she muttered.

Heat glittered in his eyes, but he locked his jaw firmly. "We're in Marrywell. What would you like to see first?"

She opened her mouth.

"And don't you dare say my cock," he warned her under his breath.

Her cheeks flushed with heat. She'd never used that word in her life—could not even recall how she'd even learned of it—but now that he'd mentioned it… Yes. She would like that very much.

But she would play along for now.

"Perhaps a stroll down High Street?" she suggested.

"Splendid." He led her from the dining room.

As they approached the exit, a footman opened the door to the street for them. Tabitha thanked him as she and Hudson swept outside.

Unlike during the matchmaking festival, the street was virtually empty. Instead of hundreds of carriages and thousands of pedestrians, there was just Tabitha and Hudson, and one or two other passers-by in the distance.

"I can hear birds chirping," she said in surprise.

"You didn't hear them yesterday?"

"Yes, in the woods. But I didn't realize how loud the matchmaking festival was. Either the birds flee whenever it's underway, or else the noise of so many carriages and people completely obliterates the sound of nature."

"Which way do you prefer it?"

"Like this," she answered without hesitation, hugging his arm in contentment. "We have the entire town to ourselves. A festival for two."

His gaze softened, and for a moment she thought he might kiss her, right here out in the open, in front of… well, no one in particular.

Instead, he asked, "Where to first?"

"The assembly rooms," she decided. "One cannot visit a matchmaking town without spending time in its ballroom."

"Do you think the assembly rooms are even open?"

"If not, there's always the outdoor venue in the botanical gardens, where the musicians play in good weather."

There was unlikely to be musicians playing at ten o'clock in the morning—or outside of festival week at all—but the town of Marrywell still seemed magical. The freshness of the air, the green trees and colorful flowers, the long rows of picturesque inns and the knowledge that thousands of hopeful hearts had found true love right here, year after year, for centuries.

To Tabitha's surprise, the doors to the assembly rooms were indeed unlocked. Hudson opened the door for her, and they slipped inside.

The large, silent rooms felt like entering a cathedral. No one was in sight. Their soft footfalls sounded thunderous. It felt a bit like two naughty children sneaking somewhere they did not belong.

When they entered the ballroom, it was completely empty... save for a piano upon the musicians' dais.

Hudson followed her line of sight. "Do you play?"

"Of course I do. I'm a 'highly accomplished' young lady. Which means my primary skills are piano-playing, embroidery, and doing as I'm told."

He sent her a skeptical look. "From what I've seen, you're dreadful at obeying. I'd hate to see your embroidery. You probably sew the openings closed when you darn stockings."

She smacked his arm. "Ladies don't darn stockings. We only sew *useless* things. Much like memorizing sonatas."

"Prove it." He nudged her toward the piano. "Play me something useless."

"Will you dance?"

"Absolutely not."

She grinned and arranged herself at the piano anyway. "Prepare to be stunned and awed by rote mimicry."

"My breath is bated," he assured her.

Tabitha placed her fingers on the keys and played. Despite her self-deprecating comments, she adored the piano. Like books, music was one of her few escapes. She could be somewhere else, *someone* else, for an hour or more at a time. No longer Lady Tabitha, betrothed since birth to a man who made her skin crawl, but the heroine of her own story. One full of fabulous adventure and sweeping scales, trilling with moments of pure joy in spite of the drum of the real world beating insistently in the background.

When she finished, she rested her hands in her lap and lifted her eyes.

Hudson was staring at her in open-mouthed wonder.

"Useless?" he repeated in disbelief. "They should be paying *you* to lead the orchestra."

She laughed and rose from the bench. "If you knew anything about music, you'd realize—"

He grabbed her hands and hauled her to him. "When will *you* realize that you aren't useless? You're worth so much more than you—"

"Of course I'm not useless. I'm use*ful*. I've been told so my entire life. That is, I'll become useful the moment I wed Lord Oldfield and fulfill my destiny. After which, I'll become useful to the viscount, in any way that he demands. A good daughter. A dutiful wife."

"That sounds dreadful. I like you better when you think for yourself and live as you please. If you were *my* wife—" He dropped her hands and turned away.

"If I were your wife?" she repeated softly, coaxingly.

He shook his head. "There's no point in finishing the sentence, is there? I might as well have said, 'If I were a fire-breathing dragon.'"

"I'm fairly certain you are one," she informed him. "Your official title might be 'man of business', but when people speak of you, it's with fear and respect. I've heard 'guard dog', 'attack dog', 'good kisser'…"

He snorted. "What do you know about that, Mrs. Snowfeather? Have you ever kissed anyone else?"

"No," she answered honestly. "Nor do I want to."

A tortured expression crossed his face. He placed her hand back on his arm and directed them toward the exit, rather than respond.

"Where to now?" he asked once they reached the pavement.

She grinned at him. "Your turn to choose."

He looked so surprised that for a second Tabitha was hurt—did he truly think her so spoilt and demanding that his own wishes and happiness were not of the least concern to her?

Just as quickly, the more likely explanation occurred to her: he was a full-time servant to an aristocratic master. And not just any lord. Viscount Oldfield, who was famously unconcerned about the desires and consent of others.

If the self-centered roué was chronically invasive and leering and rude in plain sight of an entire ballroom of his peers, heaven only knew how poorly the viscount would treat a servant considered far beneath his station in the privacy of his own home. Especially knowing that a single word from a powerful lord would be more than enough to ensure Hudson never found similar work again, if he dared to leave his master.

"Your turn," Tabitha repeated softly. "I needed this week for me, but you're here, too. This is *our* week, Mr. Snowfeather. We're on holiday together. What would you like to do next?"

He stared at her with such heat in his eyes that Tabitha blushed.

"What do I wish to do? Nothing speakable in public." He forced his gaze away and gestured down the street. "But I've always wanted to visit the brewers' field. There's no sense in going now. The vendors are long gone and—"

"We're going. Right now." She tugged him forward with a spring in her step... and a pang of sympathy in her heart. His wish was so simple. So achievable. She hated that he never had a single moment of his own to do as he pleased. Hated that *she* hadn't thought to ask his preferences a fortnight ago, when they'd both been in Marrywell, and the festival was in full swing.

Perhaps she had once indeed been spoilt and selfish after all.

When they arrived, the brewers' field was even larger than Tabitha had imagined. She'd never visited it either in all her years journeying to Marrywell, primarily because it was generally the domain of men, and not the sort of place an aristocratic young lady should be seen.

No one was here now. She and Hudson had the entire enormous field with its tall green fence of elderberry bushes all to themselves. The tents and beer stands were long gone, but dozens of huge round stone tables with matching curved stone benches dotted the empty field.

And that wasn't all.

"Look!" Tabitha pointed past the vacant tables to the furthest section of grass. "A maypole!"

The tall wooden pole stretched twelve or fifteen feet high, and was wrapped in an intricate braid of brightly colored ribbons.

"We missed the maypole dance," she said with disappointment.

Hudson chuckled. "I doubt that's true. Have

you seen the clientele of a brewers' field? I can't imagine hundreds of men frolicking with ribbons in a fertility dance by themselves, no matter how much ale they've imbibed."

"Well, *someone* put it there," Tabitha insisted.

"Therefore someone ought to dance?" he asked with amusement.

She glared at him. "Yes. It's a time-honored tradition that stretches back for centuries."

"Then I suppose we cannot stand in the way of tradition." He took her hand in his. "Come on, lady fair."

She blinked. "Really?"

Hudson tugged her toward the maypole, their steps quickly increasing from a walk to a run until they arrived, winded and laughing, at the base of the colorful pole.

"How does the dancing go?" he asked. "Are there specific figures, like a quadrille or a corn rig?"

"I don't know," she admitted. "I always imagined a maypole dance as something romantic and pagan and joyful."

"Then we'll do whatever occurs to us, and it'll be right."

"Like what?"

He answered by springing into motion, skipping around the maypole with exaggerated bounding steps whilst waving his arms about wildly, a silly expression on his handsome face.

Tabitha burst out laughing and joined him at once, skipping merrily in a way she hadn't done since she was a small child, and wiggling her arms overhead as if she were a maypole herself.

Hudson was right. This *did* feel romantic and joyful. Tabitha felt freer in this moment than she could ever recall feeling in her entire life.

It was more than the unusual sensation of peace. She felt truly happy. It bubbled within her, filling her with energy and making her light-headed with joy. The moment was carefree and perfect. She was having *fun*.

All because of the hulking giant of a man frolicking about the maypole with her.

Their windmilling hands banged together, and Hudson pulled her into his embrace. Tabitha wasted no time in wrapping her arms about his neck. She rose on her toes as his head dipped down to meet hers.

The kiss was explosive. A rainbow of colors in its own right. A dance, a frolic, as unselfconscious and joyful as their bodies. An overwhelming sense of love rushed through her, followed a frisson of panic and dread.

This was the man she wanted. Not as a pretend husband, but as a real one.

And she couldn't have him.

"What's wrong?" he murmured against her lips. "Do you want to go?"

"I never want to leave." She held him tighter. "I want to stay with you all week and forever."

"No, you don't," he said quietly. "I'm fine enough as a distraction, but nothing more permanent than that. Even without considering Oldfield… You're a lady. I'm nothing."

"You're everything," she said fiercely. "Without Oldfield, nothing would stop me from turning my back on the beau monde if it meant opening my arms and my life to you."

He shook his head. "You don't mean that. The world you were born into—"

"Has gossiped about me since before I took my first breath. Do you think my choosing a man of business would raise any more eyebrows than a newborn babe betrothed to a man older than her father?" She lifted her chin. "Regardless, what would I care? I wouldn't be around them to hear it."

He stared at her in silence for a long moment, then crushed his lips back to hers.

She kissed him as though their moments together were numbered… because they were. Without the betrothal to Lord Oldfield, Tabitha would unreservedly and eagerly spend the rest of her life with Hudson.

But she *was* promised to Oldfield. And the viscount was Hudson's employer. A man who was petty and vicious enough to enact revenge on a servant for a transgression far less bold than kissing his employer's betrothed.

Tabitha had been born doomed to a life of misery, but she needn't drag Hudson down with her. There was no path for them together. She had no business also jeopardizing the safe, secure future Hudson had built for himself out of talent and grit. He'd fought so hard and so long to rise from his humble beginnings to the respected position he held now. Pretending this week was anything more than a fantasy was a disservice to them both.

For now, they were acting out a play…

But all performances came to an end.

CHAPTER 21

$\mathcal{B}$y Friday morning, Hudson was utterly, entirely, irrevocably, head over heels in love.

Or perhaps he'd been so since the first time he laid eyes on Tabitha, and only now was finally admitting the extent of his feelings for her.

He tossed his leather satchel aside as she twirled in an abandoned field of wildflowers. He wanted her more than he'd ever wanted anything in his life. She'd all but said she felt the exact same way about him, too. They hadn't let their attraction lead to anything more than impassioned kisses, but the promise of all they could be together floated about them everywhere they went, flowering like spring and warming them like summer.

There was only one day left, and Hudson was *not* ready for their week to end.

Ever since Tabitha had said she'd prefer to have forever, Hudson had not been able to get the thought from his mind. The reasons why were obvious. The reasons why not... were obvious, too.

Her status. His lack thereof. Her betrothal. His employer. Her father. The dying wish. Her deathbed promise.

Yet there was nothing Hudson wanted more but a life with Tabitha. The possibility, rather than the impossibility, haunted his every thought. There had to be a way. There *had* to.

"Pick flowers with me," Tabitha called out, dropping to her knees amongst the wildflowers.

He joined her at once.

Hudson didn't know the least thing about flowers, wild or otherwise, much less the fine art of braiding them into a crown. But he followed Tabitha's lead, and soon they were both wearing extravagant tiaras of yellow poppies and purple violets and scarlet pimpernels.

"I crown you the Mayfair King," she informed him with a kiss on his cheek.

"You're my queen with or without a crown," he replied gruffly.

She took his hand and they tumbled backward amidst the wildflowers, their floral diadems dislodging slightly as their heads fell back against the soft grass.

Tabitha sighed happily and her eyes fluttered closed. A gentle breeze rustled her skirts and her hair.

Hudson was certain he had never beheld a more beautiful sight. Or felt more *right* than he had all week long with Tabitha. He could imagine a lifetime of lazy summer days like this one. Flowers and kisses and the simple pleasure of enjoying each other's company.

"I suppose we should head back to town and

find a tavern for supper," she murmured without opening her eyes.

He turned his own gaze toward the leather satchel he'd abandoned a few yards away. "I brought sustenance."

Her eyes opened and crinkled fondly. "Of course you did. You always think of everything."

She sat up as he crawled over to retrieve his satchel. It contained a thin red cloth, which he spread out between them in order to place the rest of the bag's contents on top: fruit, cheese, fresh bread, a bottle of wine.

Tabitha inched her way around the picnic blanket until she was seated next to Hudson, rather than across from him. Between bites of food and sips of wine, she rested her head on his shoulder, her soft warmth snuggled against him.

Hudson could almost believe they were alone in the world, and it was glorious.

It also had to come to an end. Didn't it?

Tabitha had said she wanted forever, with Hudson. Why not give it to her?

"What if we disappeared?" he asked urgently. "I could make it happen. We could vanish, never to be seen by Oldfield or anyone else in the beau monde ever again. Just you and me and endless days like this one—"

"I can't." Her voice was soft. Defeated. "I could never do that to my father."

"Then we go back," Hudson said, undaunted. "But we don't have to go through with other people's plans. Lord Oldfield—"

"—is not my primary concern. My father is.

He's been counting on me to heal an old wound my entire life. I cannot let him down."

"He's letting *you* down," Hudson said with frustration. "It's not fair of him to expect you to consign yourself to a life of misery in order to fulfill a second-hand promise he made without your knowledge or consent—"

"Since when is life fair?" she asked with a sigh, and pushed to her feet. Removing her warmth from his side. Distancing herself from his side.

Her dismissal felt like a fist to his solar plexus. Hudson had hoped that if Tabitha got to know his real self… If she saw what life could be like if she weren't a pawn in someone else's narrowminded plans… Maybe she'd choose love. Choose happiness. Choose *him*.

Now he knew: the answer was no.

Limbs heavy, he rose to his feet to escort her back to the inn for their final night in Marrywell. Tomorrow would bring the eight-hour drive to return her to her father. And Sunday morning would mark the interminable pain of losing her for the rest of his life when she joined Viscount Oldfield at the church… and became another man's wife.

CHAPTER 22

Tabitha glared at the privacy screen separating her bath from Hudson's. This was their final evening in Marrywell. The last few hours alone together. They might currently be separated in two different tubs, but there was only one bed.

And this time, she bloody well wasn't going to waste it.

As much as she longed for Hudson, she knew she couldn't have him… permanently. But they *could* have tonight.

She pushed herself up from the tub. The water was still warm, and a few soapy bubbles slid down her wet legs.

"You finished already?" came Hudson's alarmed voice from the other side of the folding screen.

He liked to be the first out of his tub, so that he could be dry and safely clothed before she withdrew from her bath.

Not tonight, damn it.

She wrapped her towel loosely around her

torso, covering herself from just above her nipples down to the top part of her thighs—and not much else. With a deep breath, she stepped around the folding screen.

Hudson let out a gurgling gasp and tried to sink further into his tub. It didn't work. He was too tall and muscled, and the tub too comically small to contain him. The water rose to his navel and halfway up his thighs. Hiding the part she was most interested in, yes. But nonetheless displaying plenty of delicious man above the soapy water.

Hudson closed his eyes as though to block out the sight of Tabitha in her damp towel.

"I'm naked," he rasped.

"So am I," she responded.

He cracked open one of his eyes a tiny sliver.

She let go of her towel, allowing it to flutter unceremoniously to the floor, where it pooled at her feet. Her naked feet. Matching the naked rest of her body. Completely exposed to his view.

He let out a groan. "If you think I'm strong enough to withstand a seduction—"

"I'm hoping you're not even going to try." She stepped forward and held out her hand. "Join me in the bed?"

His tortured expression vacillated between mulish determination and abject longing for several long seconds. At last, the stubborn set of his jaw appeared to win the internal battle.

Tabitha started to lower her outstretched hand in disappointment.

With a visible shudder, Hudson placed his large hands on the wooden rim of his tub and hauled himself to his feet.

Water sluiced down his form, rivulets running across every hard plane and muscle… including the erect member jutting from his groin. A soft gasp escaped her throat.

"Second thoughts?" he growled.

She shook her head. "None."

"Good." He grabbed his towel and began drying his form. "Or rather, probably bad. Neither of us—"

"—is going to let this opportunity pass us by," she finished, grabbing Hudson's towel from his hands and tossing it aside. "Or we'll regret it for the rest of our lives."

He gazed down at her, his eyes serious and his voice soft. "You're certain doing *this* isn't what you'll regret? There will be no undoing it afterwards."

She touched her fingertips to his bare chest. "My only regret is not starting five days ago."

His eyes flashed, and he ran a hand over his face. "Do you know anything about what you're asking?"

"I know you're wasting precious time," she grumbled. "We could be done by now if you—"

He snorted. "Making love ought to be more than just me bending you over the closest chair and having my way with you."

Her jaw dropped open. "You can make love by bending me over a chair?"

"Well… yes." He raked a hand over his wet hair, then gave her a slow, roguish grin. "And a thousand other ways I'd love to show you."

She stepped closer. "Then what are you waiting for? We only have all night."

His hands coasted lightly up her arms. "You're certain you wouldn't rather sleep?"

She shook her head. "There'll be time for that later."

"And if there's not?" he asked wickedly.

She wrapped her hands around his neck. "Even better."

He scooped her up and into his arms. Her legs locked about his hips. His erection pulsed between them.

"Remember this position," he murmured against her lips. "We might try it a little differently later."

Her lips parted in surprise. "Standing *up*?"

"I told you." He kissed the corners of her mouth. "There are at least a thousand ways to make love. Let's start with a classic."

Before she could ask more questions, he carried her into the bedroom, tossed her onto the center of the bed, then climbed atop her and captured her mouth with a kiss. Several kisses. A dizzying onslaught of kiss after intoxicating kiss.

So all-encompassing were his kisses that it took a moment for Tabitha to realize his arms weren't cradling her gently, as was previously his custom, but rather sliding worshipfully over her body.

When his palms passed lightly over her breasts, she arched up to meet him. He answered her wordless, instinctive request by concentrating his efforts there, cupping and teasing and playing.

Desire electrified her veins and pooled between her thighs. She tilted her hips, seeking, wanting.

As if he understood her needs even better than she did, he slid one of his hands down from her straining breast, over her abdomen, and between her legs.

She gasped into his mouth as his fingers found her core, stroking, circling, dipping, until the pressure building inside her could no longer be contained inside her body. She convulsed helplessly against him as shockwaves of pleasure shuddered through her.

"Can I…" she managed, trying to catch her breath. "Can I make you feel like that? With my hand?"

"Quickly and easily." His burning gaze was intense on hers. "But I only get one, and I don't want to waste it."

"You want to feel it… inside of me?"

"More ardently than words can ever express." His eyes were serious. "But are you certain that it is what *you* want?"

In response, she tucked her legs around him. "More ardently than words can express."

He kissed her unrestrainedly as he positioned his member at her entrance. "If at any time, you wish to stop…"

"I don't want to stop." She wiggled her hips in invitation. "I want to start."

His lips recaptured hers.

As he began to ease into her, a sense of fullness began to spread out from her core, followed by a frisson of alarm. He was too big. This was too much. Her body could never possibly—

A brief stab of pain startled her, and she let out a muffled cry.

Hudson froze at once, jerking his mouth away from hers, his expression horrified. "I'm sorry. I've never made love to a virgin. I was trying so hard to—"

But already the pain was gone, and just the sense of fullness remained. It wasn't bad. It might even be… good.

"I'm fine," she assured him, tilting her hips experimentally. The action caused their groins to press together, rubbing deliciously against her most sensitive area while driving his member even deeper.

He let out a groan of pleasure. "You're killing me. All I want to do is grab your hips and drive myself inside you again and again like a wild beast."

She tightened her legs about him. "Do it."

"You don't know what you're—"

"Then show me."

CHAPTER 23

*H*udson made love to Tabitha, at first slowly, deliberately, then faster and faster. He lost the ability to hold himself back. Nothing had ever felt more right.

This was what he had been born to do. This was the woman he had been placed on this earth to love and to cherish and to pleasure.

He did his best to do so now, making love not just with his cock but also with his mouth on hers, his hand on her breast, his fingers dipping between them to tease her nub as he had done before.

She responded instantly and beautifully, enveloping him in slickness and tightening around him as her kisses became more sporadic and her breath fractured by seductive little pants.

The knowledge that she was close to another orgasm almost brought him to climax himself, but he gritted his teeth and did his best to think of icy river water, mathematical equations, the distinction between parsnips and turnips—anything but the soul-buoying ecstasy of his cock sliding in and out of her like this at last.

"Hudson," she gasped. "I'm—"

The climax overtook her and whatever she'd meant to say stuttered into unintelligible syllables of wordless pleasure.

How could he defend himself against that?

His own orgasm rocketed through him, and he jerked himself free from her heat seconds before his seed spurted against her inner thigh.

"Now we'll have to bathe again," he murmured wryly.

She smiled up at him lazily, her eyes half-closed and passion-drunk. "Worth it."

Absolutely. Hudson wouldn't undo a single second of the past hour—a single moment of the past week—a single day of the years he'd spent pining after her from afar—for all the riches in the world.

Nothing had ever felt more meant to be. That it was forbidden changed nothing. Of course he knew that sleeping with his employer's betrothed was more than grounds for dismissal. Perhaps that was what Hudson wanted. To cut ties with Old-field. To bind himself to Tabitha instead.

She'd been "compromised" from the moment she ran off without a chaperone and found herself alone with him instead. Pretending to be married was scandalous enough. Acting out this most sacred and personal of rituals was more than mere playacting.

He wanted to make truth of their lie. Wanted the fiction to be real. A week of Mr. and Mrs. Snowfeather wasn't enough. A single night of love did not quench Hudson's thirst for her, but rather locked his heart to hers all the more, forging a chain of iron from each heartbeat until he was a willing prisoner of every smile, every touch of her hand, every kiss.

"Don't marry him," ripped from his throat.

She winced. "Hudson…"

Rejection flooded through him, cold and slimy and rotten. "I'm sorry. I should not have presumed to—"

"What you should do is to continue making love to me while we still can. The night is long, and we… Oh. You said we could only do it once."

Already his cock was stirring again. "I might be able to scrounge up a second wind, if you ask me very, very nicely."

She sank her hands into his hair and pressed her breasts up against his chest. "I'll do anything you like. Just tell me how to please you."

Oh, god. He didn't just have a second wind. He had a third, a fourth, a hundred. He would never sleep again, if it meant spending his every waking moment making love to Tabitha into infinity.

But he only had tonight. Eight hours. One chance, to show her with his heart and body what she would not let him say in words.

He loved her. He was hers, unconditionally.

And tomorrow morning, he would have to give her away.

CHAPTER 24

The following morning, after lingering for a bittersweet lovemaking session in bed before rising to face the day, Hudson took the reins of his barouche.

Tabitha was once again seated on the driver's perch with Hudson, rather than tucked inside the carriage. Her newly familiar curves pressed so softly against his side did not feel nearly as spontaneous and carefree as it had done when he'd first arrived in Marrywell.

They were not off on a whimsical frolic to splash in the river or dance around a maypole or chase each other through fields of wildflowers. He was driving her to a place that neither one of them wished to go.

Returning her to her father. Who would hand her over to Viscount Oldfield.

Who would make her life a living hell.

For a man who had long prided himself on being preternaturally efficient at any task his employer assigned him, no matter how difficult or distasteful, today Hudson was markedly disinclined to earn his pay.

He didn't want to ferry Tabitha back to London. He wanted to run away with her to Gretna Green, or to France, or literally anywhere the English aristocracy could not intervene in Tabitha's life, freedom, and happiness.

Now that he'd had her, for one short, perfect week, Hudson was desperate to keep her. Not just to keep her with him, but to keep her smiling. To keep her safe.

But he would deliver her to Lord Oldfield, as commanded. He'd made a promise to his employer. And, more importantly, to Tabitha.

"Well," she said, her voice shaking with obvious nervousness as the horses clopped down High Street and out of Marrywell. "I would say, 'back to our normal lives', but mine is about to change—and keep changing."

She referred not just to her rescheduled wedding tomorrow morning, but to the impending death of her father, and its accompanying year of newlywed-in-mourning.

Nor was that the only disaster awaiting her. Becoming the marital property of a selfish, capricious lord famed for his coldhearted excesses would bring a lifetime of challenges. Mockery. Pain.

Hudson's fingers clenched around the reins. A not insignificant part of him would rather quit his post, become utterly unemployable, and never earn another farthing again rather that bear witness to the hedonistic viscount tearing Tabitha down day after day until she was nothing more than a broken shadow of her former self.

But an even bigger part of him could not stomach the thought of leaving her to face such humiliation and misery alone.

As much as Hudson's heaving stomach roiled at the thought of his syphilitic employer rutting with the woman Hudson loved between visits to the viscount's whores and gaming clubs, Hudson would never leave Tabitha's side if there was the slightest chance she needed him. He would stay, for her. Do his utmost to protect her. Die a little every time she left his sight to become the viscount's temporary plaything.

As far as Hudson was concerned, going through with this farce of a marriage was the worst decision Tabitha could possibly have made. But it was her mistake to make. As much as Hudson might wish otherwise, the man she chose to marry was not up to him. He would not attempt to control her if he were her husband, which meant he certainly would make no such attempt now. If this was what she wanted, then he would do everything in his power to give it to her.

Even if it killed him inside.

CHAPTER 25

When the knock came at the door, Tabitha awoke with a start—and a painful crick in her neck. She'd fallen asleep again in the winged armchair she'd dragged into her father's sick chamber. Wracked with guilt over having run off without explanation, she'd been unable to tear herself from his side since the moment of her return the day before.

Of course, today was a new day, and she would indeed be torn from her father's side. Not for a moment or two, but forevermore. She was to present herself at the church in less than two hours to marry Lord Oldfield... who, apparently, had made multiple visits to her father's bedside during Tabitha's absence.

Not to enquire after the marquess's health, but to complain about the delayed ceremony and to request the promised dowry in advance, in consolation for the bother of having to marry her.

She sat up gingerly, massaging her stiff neck and shoulder with one hand. "Dr. Collins! Please come in. Don't mind me."

The good doctor did not look at her tangled hair and wrinkled gown aghast, but with kindness. "Shouldn't you be… elsewhere?"

Readying herself for an unwanted marriage, for example.

She stared at the doctor in anguish. "*Should* I be elsewhere? Or should I be right here with Father? He doesn't look well."

"He looks like he's sleeping peacefully."

"Too peacefully, perhaps," she fretted. "What if he doesn't wake up? What if these are my final hours to—"

"My dear Lady Tabitha," the physician interrupted gently. "I know you worry about your father, and with good reason. He *is* dying. But not today. My prognosis has not changed. He still has a few more weeks—"

"You said another month or two!"

"—which means his lordship will be more than able to attend today's wedding ceremony… *if* you allow me and the others to perform our assigned duties."

She let out a long sigh. "Of course you should do your duty. As should I. I don't know what has got into me."

"Don't you? If it is not too impertinent for me to say so, might a small part of you prefer the safety of his sickbed to the uncertainty awaiting you?"

"Make that a large part of me," she muttered.

But the truth was, it wasn't marriage that frightened her. It was the specter of a future shackled to a self-centered libertine who neither respected nor particularly wanted her. It was her dowry he needed, in order to pay his gambling debts and continue his debauched lifestyle.

Marriage to the *right* man wouldn't give her the least pause. If it was not Viscount Oldfield at the altar, but rather his man of business, Tabitha would have been coiffed and in her wedding dress since before dawn, eagerly awaiting the opportunity to dash down the aisle and into his open arms.

She forced herself up out of the chair on wooden limbs. "I suppose I should freshen up."

The marquess let out a wracking cough. His eyes flew open, and slowly focused on his daughter.

"Tabitha," he rasped. "Is it time?"

"For the wedding? Almost."

A brief smile curved his pale lips. "You're doing the right thing. I am proud to have a dutiful daughter."

She kept her mouth closed to hide her clenched teeth and nodded tightly.

Was it too much to ask to want her father to be proud of her for any reason at all besides strict obedience to his whims? Could he not be proud that she was a good person, or an accomplished pianist, or a regular sight volunteering at the local hospital? Should he not allow the possibility of a love match? Ought a father not to care about his daughter's happiness, or to consider the life in store for her if she married a gambler almost thrice her age, with a penchant for whoring and who already viewed his young bride as a barnacle to be treated with contempt and on a tight leash?

How she hated that this was the only way to

make the marquess proud. That giving her body and her life to a man she despised was the only act that would prevent her father from dying disappointed in his only daughter.

But Papa had forced a promise from her lips. Maneuvered her into this situation before she was even born. Found his only daughter an aristocratic husband, who happened to be his best friend.

And now the time had come.

She dragged herself down the corridor to her bedchamber with leaden feet. Inside the dressing room, Mary Frances awaited her with curling tongs in hand and a bleary-eyed expression that looked as though she, too, had passed the night crying.

"I wish you didn't have to do it," Mary Frances whispered.

Not: I wish you *wouldn't* do it.

But: I wish you didn't *have* to.

In all of Tabitha's twenty-two years, the only person who'd ever acted as though she ought to have a choice in the matter was… Hudson.

Who'd wanted her to choose *him*.

And, oh, how she wished she could!

Instead, she stood boneless as a rag doll as Mary Frances bathed and clothed her and dressed her hair.

"You look beautiful," her maid whispered.

Tabitha gazed at the stranger in the mirror. She looked exactly as she had one week ago, when she'd set out for the chapel the first time. But today she felt like an entirely different person. She was no longer an ignorant ingénue. Now she *knew* better. Knew exactly what she was getting herself into. Knew exactly what she was giving up. Viscerally understood the sacrifice being asked of her.

Not asked.

Demanded. Instructed. Forced.

One of the downstairs maids popped her head into the room. "The carriage is ready and waiting for you, Lady Tabitha."

"Should I pack extra clothes?" Mary Frances whispered.

Tabitha shook her head. "Not this time, I'm afraid. I shan't be running away again."

She suspected measures had nonetheless been put into place to prevent just that.

The carriage felt like a coffin. Too dark, too close, too confined. Carrying her to the death of her old life. Trundling her far away from any hope of happiness.

When the horses paused before the church, a full retinue of footmen rushed forward to escort her into the chapel. From the looks of things, she wouldn't even be allowed to duck behind a privacy screen or glance out of a window, much less visit the ladies' retiring room on her own.

Inside the chapel, two men stood at the altar—but only one of them was a true gentleman.

Society would disagree about which one that was.

Viscount Oldfield was visibly nettled. Annoyed to be here at all, when all he wanted was her dowry—and a chance to paw at her in his bed. The mere sight of him made Tabitha's gorgeous gown feel more like a strait-jacket. She was not to become a viscountess, but a prisoner of Bedlam.

Caged against her will. Inflicted with nightly visits. Expected to be *dutiful* and nothing else.

Hudson Frampton, on the other hand, looked like danger personified. His tall form and hulking muscles seemed to vibrate with barely contained rage. He did not want her to be here. He—

No, that was not quite it. His eyes melted at the first sight of her. He *did* want her here. The person he wished to kick through the closest wall was his employer. Hudson wanted to stay exactly where he was, right there at the altar. He wanted Tabitha to walk down the aisle to *him*.

He loved her, she realized in surprise and wonder. Truly, truly loved her.

He hadn't said the words, but the truth was evident in every action he made—or refrained from making. He loved her so much, he would even step aside and let her marry another man if it was what she chose to do. Because he believed she *should* have the right to choose her own future. Whether her decision aligned with what he wanted or not.

Dear God, she adored this man. If only others could see what she did. If only her father also believed women should have a voice in determining their own future.

If only it wasn't too late.

CHAPTER 26

"Step back," Viscount Oldfield snapped at Hudson. "Sit down in one of the pews."

Hudson didn't move. He couldn't. His legs were rooted to the floor, right here at the altar. Tabitha was walking toward them, her eyes on Hudson rather than his employer. No force on earth could've convinced Hudson to break that connection and walk away.

Even the priest seemed to accept Hudson's presence as part of the process. Or perhaps he'd been instructed not to allow anything or anyone to delay the ceremony a single minute longer than necessary.

The moment Tabitha was within arm's reach of the alter, the priest immediately began to speak. "Dearly beloved, we are gathered together here…"

Hudson blocked out the horrendous words and concentrated instead on the pounding of his heart and the beautiful woman standing before him. Oh, the words themselves weren't horrific. It was the thought of Tabitha belonging to the viscount that was the tragedy.

He wanted these words to be spoken to *him*, not to his employer. Not because he wanted to possess Tabitha. The opposite. Hudson wanted to pledge his own life to her. To make any vow she asked for. To belong to *her*, wholly and completely, now and always, from this day forward.

"...this man and this woman in holy matrimony..." the priest droned on.

Tabitha's eyes were still locked on Hudson's. As if the only way she was managing to stomach the ceremony at all was because she, too, was imagining Hudson was her groom, and Viscount Oldfield the insignificant fly buzzing about them.

Vaguely, Hudson was aware of the others in the audience. The Marquess of Brigsby, in his wheeled chaise, surrounded by maids and footmen and his physician. Tabitha's lady's maid, Mary Frances. Brigsby's own man of business, who would serve as witness to the ceremony, just as Hudson was meant to do.

No family. No friends. Either they hadn't been invited, or they too saw this mésalliance for the abomination it was, and refused to bear witness to a young woman coerced against her will to become property of a man who wasn't even trying to hide his annoyance at having to saddle himself with a bride just to get his hands on her money.

Hudson could barely keep himself from reaching for Tabitha and whisking her out of there.

The priest closed his Bible and raised his voice. "If anyone here should know any impediment, why ye may not be lawfully joined together in matrimony, ye must now confess it. For on this day—"

"I do," Hudson burst out, shocking the entire chapel into silence. *Speak now or forever hold your peace* was a formality, not an invitation. But he could contain himself no longer.

Dozens of wide eyes darted his way in unison. But the only eyes that mattered to Hudson were those belonging to Tabitha.

"This injustice cannot continue," he said. Softly, firmly. Not a shout, but a voice that carried throughout every corner of the chapel. "Not this day, and not any day. Stop the wedding. Stop all of this. It should never have started."

"Now see here—" began Lord Oldfield, his cheeks mottled with anger.

Hudson whirled on him. "I've seen everything I need to see. Thanks to standing in your shadow for over a decade, I've seen the careless disregard you hold for other people, for women in general, for this woman in specific. She doesn't want you. You don't even want her. And you certainly don't want to heal old family rifts. All you care about is her dowry."

Gasps ricocheted throughout the chapel.

Viscount Oldfield vibrated with embarrassment. "My financial circumstances are not the business of this congregation. As my man of business, you—"

"—are not your anything anymore," Hudson interrupted. "Consider this my resignation. And, if the lady agrees, a new beginning."

Tabitha's eyes widened. Hudson turned his attention to her.

"This isn't the future you want," he said softly. "So don't take it. Do you know what matters more than an agreement someone else made before you were even born? *You* do. *You* matter. This is your life, Tabitha. You're the one most impacted by whatever does or doesn't happen here today. You shouldn't be given the power to decide for yourself. You should already have it. You *do* have it, if you're brave enough to act on it."

"Act…how?" she whispered.

"Do you want to marry Lord Oldfield?" he asked quietly.

She froze, her eyes enveloping him for a long moment. Silence grew about them, thick as gravy. Tabitha sucked in an audible breath, then gave a short, decisive shake of her head.

Gasps echoed around the chapel.

"Then don't do it." He grasped her hands.

"Now, wait just a minute, Mr. Frampton—" the marquess rasped.

"No, *you* wait," Hudson said, earning even more shocked responses from the rapt audience. "Your daughter has spent her entire life doing her level best to please you. She wants to be dutiful. She wants you to be proud of her. But what about your duty as a father? Should you not be proud of this wonderful woman you've raised, without obligating her to submit to being a pawn or a plaything to a man who spent the wee hours of this very morning gambling and whoring on credit, because he sees your daughter as a purse rather than as a person?"

Tabitha's eyes filled with tears.

Hudson pressed her fingers to his lips. "I'm sorry. I didn't mean for you to find out like this—"

"I've known," she managed in humiliation. "I just didn't know that everybody else knew, too."

The marquess harrumphed. "I'm certain you're overstating the extent of the matter, but… What a man does on his own time is neither your nor Tabitha's concern."

"That's right," Lord Oldfield put in. "Just because I have a few flaws—"

"Your flaws are not of Lady Tabitha's concern… if she doesn't marry you." Still holding Tabitha's hands, Hudson dropped to his knees and gazed up at her beseechingly. "You deserve a man who wants you. *I* want you. You deserve a man who loves you. *I* love you. You deserve a man who would spend his last breath in praise of you, or protecting you, or picking wildflowers with you. Anything that brings a smile to your face."

She sucked in a shuddering breath.

He forged on. "Pleasing you is no sacrifice. It is how I will gladly spend the rest of my life, if you let me. Which should be your decision. If you want me, you need only to say so. And if you do not want me, again, you need only to say so. All I desire is for you to have anything and everything *you* desire. That's what love is."

"I love you, too," she whispered.

Hope shot through him. "Then do something about it. Leave here, with me. Be my wife. Let me dedicate the rest of my days to ensuring every moment of your life is full of joy."

Her voice wobbled. "I would love that. But we're in the middle of a ceremony…"

"An easily resolvable situation," he promised. "To be clear, that was a yes?"

She bit her lip, then grinned. "An enthusiastic yes. I just don't see how—"

"Watch carefully." He dropped her hands and grabbed her waist instead, tossing her over his shoulder as he pushed to his feet.

She let out a surprised squeal, then giggled against his back.

"Highly irregular," blurted the stunned priest.

"Irregular!" snapped Viscount Oldfield. "You cannot take my bride! *Or* quit your post! How will I become solvent again without you to—"

"Huzzah!" Mary Frances called out, clapping her hands in delight. "Someone get the door!"

One of the footmen immediately did just that, twisting the handle and pulling the door open wide.

Hudson marched down the aisle with his future bride over his shoulder. Scattered applause broke out from the maids and footmen. The Marquess of Brigsby stared at them with his mouth hanging open. Mary Frances tossed flower petals at them as they passed.

When they were back out in the sunlight, Hudson placed Tabitha on her feet. Her hair was mussed and her gown wrinkled beyond repair. He had never seen her look more beautiful.

"Where to now?" she asked. "Gretna Green?"

"Unnecessary." He retrieved a piece of paper from inside his waistcoat.

She unfolded it in shock. "You secured a marriage license?"

"A good man of business is always prepared for anything," he informed her with a straight face.

"How about an escape vehicle?"

Hudson lifted his fingers. Before he could snap, his barouche arrived from around the corner. He grinned at Tabitha. "You were saying?"

"A change of clothes?" she asked hopefully.

"You'll find a new wardrobe in a trunk in the back."

"Breakfast?"

"In the basket on the rear seat."

"Happy ever after?"

"Ah." He took her hand in his and kissed her cheek. "That's something we'll have to find together."

And so they did.

CHAPTER 27

*L*ater that afternoon, after a leisurely picnic breakfast, Tabitha and Hudson took a beautiful spring stroll through the park… during which Tabitha gradually grew more and more discomfited.

It wasn't that she thought she'd made a mistake —thanks to Hudson, she knew she hadn't. She loved him and he loved her. They made each other *happy*. There was no doubt in either of their minds that they were meant to be together.

As for Lord Oldfield's feelings on the matter… Tabitha couldn't bring herself to truly regret having jilted him at the altar, not once, but twice. She should never have been present at that altar to begin with. No one had asked her if she wanted to marry him. She'd been assigned the task before she was old enough to speak for herself, and even after she'd gained the capacity to express herself eloquently, nobody had cared about her wishes.

Until Hudson. Who was glancing down at her now with love… and concern.

"What is it?" he asked softly.

"Father," she admitted. "I don't regret choosing you over Oldfield, but I cannot bear the thought of my father dying both angry and disappointed with me. I have to see him one more time."

"Of course you do," Hudson said without hesitation. "As many times as you please. Shall I take you to him now?"

Relief eased a little of her anxiousness. "Would you?"

"Without delay." He spun about on the walking path and led her out from the flowering trees and back to his carriage.

In the short fifteen-minute drive from the park to her father's town house, Tabitha's disquiet increased. What must her father be thinking? What would he say when he saw her? Worse, what if he *wouldn't* see her? Or—God help her—what if he *couldn't* see her, and her picnic in the park meant she would arrive too late for any hope of reconciliation?

Hudson paused the horses in front of the crescent and turned to Tabitha with his eyes full of compassion. "Shall I come in with you?"

She shook her head. "I must do this by myself."

He kissed her forehead. "Take your time. I'll be here waiting, no matter how long it takes. And I'll bring you back as often as you like."

"Thank you," she said, and meant it. The sensation of being heard and respected and cared for was still new and heady. Yet there was no doubt in her mind that Hudson would be right here in this carriage even if she didn't leave her father's side until two o'clock in the morning.

The question was whether Father would admit her into the house at all.

She presented herself at the door with trepidation, smoothing the skirts of the pretty green day dress Hudson had procured for her. Unlike her wedding gown, this dress did not feel like a straitjacket. It felt like love. And caring. And thoughtfulness.

She hoped the streak of good fortune would continue a few minutes more.

When Yarrow, the butler, answered the door, his eyes widened at the sight of her.

"Lady Tabitha." Yarrow paused. "Are you still Lady Tabitha?"

Her cheeks heated and she nodded quickly. "Mr. Frampton and I haven't married yet… but we will."

Yarrow stepped aside. "Come in."

Her shoulders sagged in relief. "He hasn't barred me from entry?"

"I have heard no such orders." The butler gave her a conspiratorial wink. "And my aging mind would promptly forget them, even if I were so commanded."

"Thank you, Yarrow." She flashed him a grateful smile and then raced up the familiar stairs before the order *could* come down from above.

When she reached her father's sickroom, Tabitha paused to collect her breath. The door was ajar, and she could hear voices inside: the physician Dr. Collins and his patient, the marquess.

Her father was still alive.

Whether he'd consent to see her or not…

Instead of knocking on the door, she boldly

pushed it open. Both men glanced in her direction, the physician's hushed words cutting off mid-sentence.

Tabitha didn't say anything foolish like, *Am I interrupting?* Obviously she was interrupting. Once upon a time, it wouldn't have mattered. Once upon a time, she would have been seated at her father's side to begin with, and be the one to answer the door to admit the doctor, rather than the other way round.

The physician's eyes were kindly. "I'll give you two a moment alone."

Tabitha's gaze darted from Dr. Collins to her father, who had said nothing since her unexpected arrival. His face was impassive even now, his unfocused blue eyes gazing at nothing rather than bothering to so much as glance at her face.

Dr. Collins closed the door as he exited.

Tabitha immediately took the empty chair next to the head of her father's bed. She reached for her father's hand, then thought better of it, and folded her fingers tightly in her lap instead.

She took a deep breath. "Father…"

His eyes slashed over to her at last, glinting like chips of ice in the afternoon sun. "How *could* you, Tabitha?"

"Oldfield doesn't even want me," she burst out. "He wants my dowry. Give it to him, if it makes you happy."

The marquess coughed. "You haven't wed that bulldog?"

"Not yet, and his name is Hudson. He loves me, Father. And I, him. Ours is a love match—"

"You were already betrothed."

"I never asked to be!"

"*I* decided," he rasped. "It was not up to you."

"Should it not have been?" she asked plaintively. "Should my needs and happiness not have any bearing on your decisions at all?"

"Of course they do. But all acts should be performed in service of the greatest good. Inconveniencing one person—"

"Inconveniencing!"

"—to reunite two entire families, torn apart for generations—"

"Father, that's not what would happen!"

"Of course it would. Such a sacrifice would prove—"

"—nothing at all," she interrupted passionately. "When you were a child, perhaps the feud was indeed the demon destroying peace as you knew it, but decades have passed since then. *Our* side of the family certainly isn't torn asunder. There is only you and me—"

"And if you would not do it for us, then at least think of Lord Oldfield and the rest of the Medfords, who have also been waiting for—"

"Nothing whatsoever. With the exception of the viscount, they await nothing, and want for nothing. I approached them myself at a ball, and do you know what they said? They cautioned me *against* this foolish betrothal. They invited me to visit any time I pleased. There is no rift, Father. It's a new generation now. We can mend fences with a smile, not a grand sacrifice."

Her father frowned. "Nonsense. Oldfield would have told me if there was no longer urgent need for an olive branch."

"Would he have?" she asked softly. "Are you certain?"

A wrinkle of doubt crossed her father's face.

Tabitha leaned forward urgently. "Did you know he was a gambler and a libertine?"

"Many aristocratic men play at cards and indulge in the occasional discreet affair—"

"Did you know he gambled away every penny of the fortune Hudson amassed for him, and half of my impending dowry, too? Did you know before Hudson announced it that he spent the hours before our vows to God in a brothel, rutting with whores?"

Her father closed his eyes as if blocking out the sun.

"You did know," she whispered in shock. "You knew, and you were going to give me to him anyway."

"I had heard rumors." His chest rattled. "But the greater good—"

"To the devil with your ideals if they do not encompass your own family! What kind of man cares more about an impulsive promise made decades ago than he cares for his own daughter?"

Her father's eyes flew open. "That's not true. I love you, Tabitha."

She stared at him. "You've never said so before."

"I didn't think it necessary."

"Didn't think it *necessary*?" she choked out. "I have spent my life trying to earn your love. Being the person you wanted me to be. Giving up hobbies I adored, accepting an unwanted betrothal to a man who holds me in contempt. Never once did you give me any reason to believe I was ever good enough for you, much less acceptable just as I am."

Belated understanding crossed her father's face at last. Understanding and… guilt.

"The rift that needs mending," he rasped in horror, "is between the two of us."

Tabitha gave a jerky nod. "I have been trying to cross the bridge to you my entire life. No matter how hard I tried, I never made it into your good graces."

"You've never *left* my good graces," the marquess said gruffly. "I was hard on you because I knew your intelligence and your capacity for good are limitless. You were already the best daughter a man could be blessed to have. I simply pushed you to be even better…"

Tabitha's fingers tightened in her lap, turning the knuckles white.

"…when I shouldn't have," her father finished. "I should have told you how much you meant to me. And I should not have allowed my debt to Oldfield coerce me into sacrificing the greatest treasure I've ever had."

"My dowry?" she said, her voice wobbling.

"My daughter. Oldfield may have saved my life, but it is a father's duty to give his daughter a life of her own." He held out his trembling arms. "Come here, if it's not too late."

"It will never be too late." She threw herself into her father's embrace as gently as she could, pressing her wet cheek against his nightshirt as he held her close for the first time.

"I don't want to lose you," he murmured into her hair.

"I don't want to lose you, either," she choked out against the linen of his shirt.

"Where does your abductor intend to whisk you off to tonight?"

"A hotel, I imagine. We certainly cannot return to his rooms at Viscount Oldfield's. But don't worry. It won't take long for Hudson to find us a new home—"

"I'm not worried, because he needn't bother looking any longer. This house becomes yours the day I die. But it's already your home, here and now. Where is the lucky groom?"

"Outside, in his carriage."

"Well, tell him to come inside, and stop acting like a stablehand in front of my neighbors. If you're going to marry him, then this is his home, too."

Tabitha gasped and sat up enough to stare into her father's face. "You bless the wedding?"

"Bless it? I'll be there in the first row." He coughed over her shoulder. "You'd better do it soon, though. Is this afternoon too early?"

"Hudson procured a regular license, not a special license," she explained with regret. "He can do almost anything, but since he's not a lord—"

"*I* am," her father said gruffly. "I'm owed favors from half this town. They might as well settle their debts before I die. Go and tell your groom to freshen up and comb his hair. He's getting married within the hour."

"Thank you, Papa," Tabitha whispered.

"It's the least a father can do." He gave her a self-deprecating half-smile. "See? You were the perfect olive branch after all."

EPILOGUE

One month later

Hudson waited until the last of the day's clients had been escorted out of his home office before he collapsed backward in his armchair and let out a sonorous sigh.

"Long day?" asked Tabitha with sympathy.

He waggled his eyebrows at his wife. "Desperate for a long night."

She batted her eyelashes at him. "Another sleepless night planned? However will you concentrate tomorrow, if you spend your bedtime hours engaged in vigorous activity?"

He sprang up from his chair and pulled her into his arms. "How can I concentrate on anything but you right now, when we're alone in a room with no interruptions and nothing to—"

A knock sounded on the door.

Hudson let out a groan, flopping his shoulders against the closest bookcase and flinging an arm over his grimacing face with melodramatic flair.

"What now?" he demanded as the door creaked open.

"Dinner is served," murmured an apologetic footman.

Semi-apologetic. With a hint of constrained amusement, as if the rotter knew very well how Hudson would prefer to dine this evening.

And was not nearly apologetic enough.

"There, there." Tabitha kissed Hudson on his cheek. "We can resume after dessert."

"I want you for dessert," he growled.

"I'll consider the merits of your petition," she replied pertly, and skipped toward the door before he could haul her back into his arms.

He chased after her.

When he reached the corridor, she hooked her arm through his and grinned at him. "I'm proud of you, you know."

"I'm proud of *you*," he countered.

Thanks to his recent marriage well above his league to Tabitha, and also thanks to the far reaches of his new father-in-law's influence, Hudson interfaced with members of the ton every single day.

Not as an aristocrat himself, but as a trusted advisor. His client list contained dozens of well-known names, from lords to widows. Hudson aided each one of them with personalized advice in choosing the right investments and managing their funds.

"You could've kept my money," Tabitha said.

He nibbled her earlobe. "I wanted you, not your dowry."

Instead, Hudson had asked the marquess to

place the funds into a trust in Tabitha's name, so that every farthing belonged to her, and only to her. Hudson's initial thought had been to teach his wife how to invest the balance, so that if anything happened to him, Tabitha could carry on without financial fear.

To his delight, she'd far surpassed the lessons he'd planned to bestow, and had become his right hand in his new venture—his own personal woman-of-business, as it were.

According to Tabitha, female clients preferred her advice because Hudson's rough looks and brusque manner were off-putting at best. But that was only part of the truth.

The fact was, Tabitha's cleverness and intuitive grasp of the market meant that she gave legitimately good advice. It wouldn't be long at all before Hudson was begging her to accept a role as full partner in his new firm.

"At least this isn't another dinner party," he grumbled.

His wife swatted his shoulder. "I thought you liked our dinner parties! That's how you landed half of your current clients."

"Every last one of them takes up time that I could be spending with you."

"You *are* spending time with me," she reminded him. "I have a desk of my own, right there in your office, and at dinner parties I sit at the table by your side."

"Yes, but you're not naked on top of it," he muttered. "I must simply imagine it vividly whilst pretending to listen to other people prattle on."

"If you're very nice at tonight's dinner, I'll consider tidying the paperwork off your desk so that it can be employed in a less boring fashion," she promised him.

He brightened at once and kissed her lips. "It's a deal."

Hudson's life and calendar had never been so full. Not every member of the ton was willing to accept such an unconventional couple into their exalted echelons, in light of Hudson's humble birth. But enough of them were true friends of Lady Tabitha—or long repulsed by Viscount Old-field—that Tabitha and Hudson had no shortage of cozy parties to attend or acquaintances to invite over.

His wife squeezed his arm. "Now, hurry up. Father's waiting."

Hudson grinned despite himself. The marquess had good days and bad days, but had been holding steady ever since Tabitha moved in to stay. Father and daughter were getting along better than ever. All of their final memories of each other would be happy ones.

As would the memories Hudson and Tabitha made with each other, and their own future family.

One bed—or desk—at a time.

THANK YOU

AND SNEAK PEEKS

ABOUT THE AUTHOR

Erica Ridley is a *New York Times* and *USA Today* best-selling author of witty, feel-good historical romance novels, including THE DUKE HEIST, featuring the Wild Wynchesters. Why seduce a duke the normal way, when you can accidentally kidnap one in an elaborately planned heist?

In the *12 Dukes of Christmas* series, enjoy witty, heartwarming Regency romps nestled in a picturesque snow-covered village. After all, nothing heats up a winter night quite like finding oneself in the arms of a duke!

Two popular series, the *Dukes of War* and *Rogues to Riches*, feature roguish peers and dashing war heroes who find love amongst the splendor and madness of Regency England.

When not reading or writing romances, Erica can be found eating couscous in Morocco, ziplining through rainforests in Central America, or getting hopelessly lost in the middle of Budapest.

$\sim$

Let's be friends! Find Erica on:
www.EricaRidley.com

www.ingramcontent.com/pod-product-compliance
Lightning Source LLC
Chambersburg PA
CBHW061442210726
48287CB00007B/2312